CONFESSIONS OF A SMALL TOWN FLORIST

by Aubrey Mathis

CONFESSIONS OF A SMALL TOWN FLORIST

I turned the key in that old door on that Monday morning with all the optimism the world had to offer. As I walked into the hundred-year-old building, a shiver went down my spine. Was it the excitement of this venture, or a sign of things to come?

"Hello, Susanna's Flower Shop, how can I help you?" I said with all the enthusiasm of a child getting ready to tell Santa their Christmas wish list. My first call as a business owner.

"Who is this? Where is Judith?" Said the caller in a not-so-happy-to-hear-me voice."

"This is Susanna, I am the new owner of the flower shop. Judith is no longer in business. Is there anything I can help you with today?" I replied determinedly to win her love and affection.

"Well, I doubt it. Judith is my very good friend and knew my exact order. Will you talk to her, tell her Mary Edith called?" And, with an aggravated sigh, she slammed the phone down.

WOW! Well, that sucked. My first call and I did not get an order. Here I sit, all alone in a new town, a SMALL town, with a cooler full of the prettiest blooms you can imagine, their fragrances filling this old building, and the first call I get is for the former owner. What in the hell have I done?

~

"I CANNOT LIVE LIKE THIS ANYMORE, ETHAN. I expect to be treated with respect and dignity and not like some dog you found in the street who is just happy he's not standing in the rain. This immature crap that goes on every single night with you has to end or I'm out of here, and this time I AM DEAD SERIOUS!"

"Yeah right, Susanna, you're a lifelong quitter. What the hell do you have and where could you possibly go and make it without me? I am your everything, BABY DOLL! Now, get that fine little booty into the kitchen and get me a beer. Oh, and, honey, do not die on your way there with all that seriousness you got going on."

As I lay awake in bed that night, sick of myself and of the life I was living, I knew I could not continue this fake love. Restless with uncertainty, I got up and started googling. The words typed themselves out: "How to leave a horrible relationship." Page after page of hotline numbers and self-help gurus popped up. *This isn't it*, I thought. *I know how to leave…. I just get in my car and leave. I need to know where to go.*

The google bar read, "Where to live that is peaceful, friendly, and easy going." Right underneath was an advertisement, "FLOWER SHOP FOR SALE in the most peaceful, easy going, friendliest town in the WHOLE US of A." *Is this a joke ad? Like if I click on it, a naked lady will pop up and my computer will crash,* I thought to myself. Something inside me said to do it, see what it was, and GET OUT OF THERE! So, I took the bait, and there it was…a picture of a town that time had forgotten. The old buildings were still standing erect, but how was a big question.

"Florist retiring after forty years in the business. Building and all supplies for sale! 900 square feet of historic brick walls, metal-tiled ceiling, and the oldest chandelier in the county hangs in the building on the main street in Cartman, Texas." Oldest chandelier in the county.... well then, why not?

That next morning, almost gleefully I got up and called the realtor for the flower shop.

"Cartman Real-idy, this is Annie."

"Hi Annie, my name is Susanna Hightower, and I am interested in the flower shop you have listed for sale."

"Uhhuh, so whatcha you wanna know, hun?"

"Well, um, I guess, how much is the asking price?"

"It's twenty-five thousand dollars, hun, and that includes the building and the florist supplies. Miss Judith is a dear sweet friend of mine, so I'm not charging a commission. Her husband recently passed, and she is ready to retire. This town won't be the same without her," says Annie mournfully. *Geez, lady, what a way to try and make a sale. Ever heard of Tony Robbins? Maybe you need some Business Mastery classes.* As Annie gets her wits back, she says, "Well, hun, you interested?"

"Um, yes ma'am, I think I might be. Do you have any video of the building, and can you send me the P&Ls for the past five years?"

"No, no video, and I am pretty doubtful Judith has anything like that for records. This isn't a fancy, uptown flower shop, hun. This is a small-town business. People don't get into all the big business number stuff like that down here. The only reason this listing is even on that world wide web thing is because my nephew is training under me to get his real-state license, and he wants to get 'famous' and have the world see his picture on the enter-net. I can get Judith to just write something up and call you back with it." Call me back with it? *Hey lady, why don't you just strap it to a pigeon and send it that way? How about email?*

"Ok, great. I look forward to that call. Annie, I will also be looking for a place to rent, since I am not from the area. I don't need anything big, just a bed and a bathroom, something affordable but clean. Do you have any listings I can look at?"

"Yea, I can find you something," replied Annie. "I'll holler back atchya in a day or so." *I'll be listening for the holler.*

"Thank you, have a nice day." Click.

~

"Oh, Susanna, oh won't you bring to me a cold beer in a koozie and a whiskey just for me?" Ethan sang as he walked in the door. Looking at him, you would see the typical, handsome, professional man. A man of prestige who carries a briefcase and works on Wall Street. But the wolf of Wall Street isn't is a wolf at all, no. He is a sheep. A coward in wolf's clothing. He is a tiny fragment of a man on the inside, but outside he is a massive force.

It was his suit and his long line of bullcrap that swayed my heart to move from my loft above the Japanese food restaurant—where I was also working my way to the top of the managerial chain—and into his cold, marbled, black and white condo. This sheep in wolf's clothing had taken away my pride little by little, moment by moment, until that night he came in demanding his beer and whiskey.

BEER AND WHISKEY! What kind of refined man drinks beer and whiskey every single night? And what kind of man sits and yells obscenities at the woman he is supposed to love? Not a man at all.

After three years of hearing him sing that stupid song he thought was so hilarious, I'd had enough. I called the bank the next day, even before Annie called me back with the profit and losses, and wired the twenty-five thousand dollars to Judith Markley, signed the deed to a hundred-year-old building, and googled "HOW TO BE A FLORIST."

"Ethan, I told you I was dead serious, I'm leaving. I bought a business in Texas, and tomorrow I am flying out to start a new life. I really hope you get the help you need." He laughed so hard he spilled his whiskey.

"You? You bought a business…in Texas? And you...you are leaving me tomorrow?"

"Yes, that is what I said."

"Oh Susanna, sweetie, you will never survive. It's you that needs the help, dear. My advice is that you watch your back for knives because you have no idea who will stab you. You trust too many people, and you do not have what it takes to be a business person. Good night, Oh Susanna. Or should I say, Good Bye, Oh Susanna."

From New York to Texas, this was it. My new life, my new career, my new peaceful, relaxed, friendly-living old town. As I got my luggage and looked for the baby blue, four-door sedan Annie told me she would be in, I started to tear up and second-guess my decision. I was a lifelong quitter, Ethan was right. I didn't finish college. I had quit more jobs in one year than most people their whole life. In fact, the only consistent thing I ever did was stay in the relationship I had with Ethan.

"STOP!" I screamed at myself. "YOU CAN AND YOU WILL DO THIS. This is your time to make a life for yourself, to chase your dreams, open your business, and find the love you deserve."

Just as I had drifted off into picking out curtains for my kitchen in a house I did not have, and cooking supper for a husband I had yet to meet, I was startled by my own name.

"Susanna? Susanna Hightower from New York?" the familiar raspy voice said. I now recognized the voice and finally had a face to match it to.

Annie Deets was exactly who I'd thought she'd be. We had yet to meet face-to-face after our first call, and things had moved progressively fast. I had the cash to pay for the flower shop from a small inheritance my grandmother had left me when she passed away a year before. My grandmother's only stipulation: "Susanna," she said before she died, "use this to fund your dreams, no matter how big or small. My only regret is that I never chased my dreams. Life will happen and, in a blink, your opportunities will be over. Please don't buy a silly car or a fancy trip. And please, Susanna, DO NOT SPEND THIS ON A MAN!"

I knew I was doing the right thing as I held out my hand to formally introduce myself to the town realtor.

"Hi, Annie. I am Susanna Hightower. Thank you so much for picking me up from the airport. I hope it wasn't too much of a hassle."

"Oh, what is my day if I don't have to tend to a little hassle? I'm used to it," replied Annie. One thing was for sure, you never had to wonder what Annie Deets was thinking.

As I got into the four-door, baby blue sedan, I could taste the smell of cigarettes mixed with the sweet, sweet aroma of Vanilla Fields perfume. *Dear sweet Jesus, how long can I hold my breath*? I thought.

"So, Annie, tell me. Have you lived in Cartman long?"

"All my living days. I was born in the same house I live in now. My granddaddy was Bill Cartman. He was the first mayor of the town. It was known as Beedlesville before it was renamed after he passed. He formed the first city council and incorporated the town. Since then we've grown some, but for the most part we've stayed the same. Not too many changes. Not too many newcomers. People come then they leave…. But I'm sure you will do ok. Judith grew a fine business with her flower shop. Yes, she is going to be missed. That's for certain…."

As Annie snapped back from her mourning over the loss of Judith's flower shop, she said, "What about you, Susanna? This seems like a big leap you are taking. I mean, do you have experience in the flower business? How long have you been a florist?"

"Oh," with a nervous laugh I replied, "I actually do not have experience in the flower shop business, but I do have managerial experience. I am hoping to hire a florist and just run the business side of the flower shop." Annie looked at me as if what I just said was a confession to murder. I smiled, waiting for a response.

She chuckled, rolled her eyes, and lit a cigarette. Through the cigarette in her teeth, she said, "Susanna, let me give it to you straight. I probably should have talked you out of purchasing the flower shop, but since I wanted to help Judith get out from under it as soon as possible, I had to look out for my friend first. Cartman is an old, set in their way kinda town. When I told ya it hasn't changed much, it's not because we haven't had young folks like you come in with a dream and a prayer of flipping the town. It's because we don't want change, and we make sure it doesn't happen.

"So, before you *hire*"—she says with air quotes—
"yourself a florist, you need to see how long you stay in
business. That's my advice to you, from one business
owner to the next."

I felt as though the wind had just been knocked out
of me. I tried to inhale, but the cigarette smoke from
Annie's exhaling went down my windpipe and, dear sweet
Lord, I was choking, coughing up a lung.

This was it. I was going to die. I was going to die in
a town where no one liked me though they hadn't even met
me, in a four-door, baby blue sedan, choking on Vanilla
Fields perfume and cigarette smoke from a lady who sold
me a business who just confessed she shouldn't have sold it
to me because of the "townspeople" who evidently went
after newcomers like they were ogres that needed to be run
out of town.

WHAT HAVE I DONE, I asked myself for the second time that day?

~

For the past 6 months I had planned and researched everything there was to know about running a flower shop and there I sat at the front counter after that first call, I couldn't believe that I had made the most idiotic choice a person, a woman, could make. I mean, was life with Ethan as bad as I made it out to be? Maybe it was all in my head. I mean, sure he drank at night to unwind…he had a stressful job. I was supposed to be his partner. Was I being selfish by not tending to him when I got home? My job wasn't really that stressful. *Seriously, I wonder if he would take me back.*

Ding ding clanked the cowbell on the front door. *Get it together, Susanna. It's your first real-life customer.*

"Excuse me," said the most masculine voice I'd ever heard in my life.

"Hi, come on in. I'm Susanna. I'm the new owner. Can I help you?"

That would be the first time I laid eyes on who I could only pray was my future husband. And just as I was naming our unborn children, he said, "Yes ma'am." *Oh my God, did he just call me ma'am? My heart cannot take this kind of charm.*

"Yes ma'am, I need to send some flowers." *Yuck, he has a girlfriend or, worse, a wife already, who is probably flawless and beautiful, and now I have to send the luckiest girl in the world flowers from Prince Charming.*

"Ok, do you want to send roses? Nothing says 'I love you' like red roses. I can make a really romantic vase of red roses for you." I had googled how to arrange roses so many times I knew I could handle this order.

He laughed, and when he did, I swear my heart stopped. That smile, those teeth. Where in the world did, he come from? Heaven? He had to be an angel in a white tee-shirt because I had seen handsome men before, even men who made a living with their looks, but this man made them look like little boys. But why was he laughing at me?

"No ma'am, nothing romantic. Though I do need them to be special. This lady does have my heart." *Ok, what does that mean*, I thought. How can a woman have your heart, but you don't want to be romantic?

"Well, how about daisies? Daisies are my personal favorite, and I can add some lilies to make it extra special. What's this special lady's name and address?"

"Oh, I don't need them delivered. If you don't mind, I can come back and pick them up. I will take them to her myself. I work right down the road at the feed store."

"Ok, I can do that. I will have them ready by four thirty. Will be that be okay?"

"Yes ma'am, that will be perfect."

"Perfect. And what was your name…?"

"K.C." he said with a smile that made me want to jump over the counter and kiss him like Rhett Butler kissed Scarlett O Hara. *Get it together, Susanna. He's a customer— your only customer! —and he's picking up flowers for a special lady WHO. HAS. HIS. HEART.*

I spent the whole day on that arrangement of daisies and lilies, not only because I had no clue as to what I was doing and I couldn't get it to look exactly like the lady did in the video, but also because it was sadly my only order for the day. The phone did not ring except for the old, aggravated lady looking for Judith, and the cowbell only clanked one time when Mr. Wonderful walked through this morning.

At four twenty I had the arrangement ready. I was so proud of the final product I took around thirty pictures of it, from all angles. I would need it for my social media marketing and any ads I would run in the local newspaper.

When I heard the door open and the clanking of the bell, my stomach flipped a little.

"Hi, K.C. your arrangement ready for your special lady. Would you like a card or a teddy bear to go with it?"

"No thank you, ma'am! The flowers will be just fine. How much do I owe?" *Just your love until death do us part will be fine*, I thought.

"Umm, with tax, let me see. It will be…" *Oh my gosh, I can't even do simple math! I look like a moron,* "thirty-five eighty-nine."

"Here is forty. Keep the change. These are the prettiest flowers I have seen in a long time," said K.C.

"Thank you. Oh wow, geez, you really don't have to. I have change."

"Susanna was it?" he asked. I smiled at the sound of my name on his lips. It was as if the skies opened and the angels sang it out loud. "These are beautiful, and this town is lucky to have you bring such beauty to it." As he smiled his charming smile, I saw something mischievous this time, flirty even. Was Mr. Wonderful flirting with me while holding the flowers I made for his special lady who has his heart???

"Well, thank you, K.C. I truly appreciate that, and I hope you come back."

As he walked out of the building and I locked the door and turned off the open sign, I couldn't help but think of what he said. The town was lucky for me to bring beauty to it. That night, I stayed up all night making the happiest, friendliest arrangements, all with a handwritten card introducing myself to the business owners of the town. If I could get them to like me and see the value I could bring to the town, surely, they wouldn't come after me with lit torches and kerosene. Maybe this town wasn't as harsh as Annie made it out to be. Perhaps it was ready for a change.

~

That next morning as I walked into my flower shop, I did not have the same girlish excitement as the day before. That morning I walked in with the confidence of a businesswoman. I bought this building, I signed on the dotted line, and I committed myself to make this work. I walked straight to the coolers, loaded up the arrangements I made the night before into a little red wagon left at the back of the building, and headed down the main street of Cartman, Texas. If they were not going to send the welcome wagon to me, then I was going to bring it to them!

First stop, Cartman City Hall.

As I walked into the newest building in the town, it was almost as if I hadn't stepped back in time. The wall had a mural of the original city hall, the floors were marble and the countertops granite. This building defiantly didn't fit the mold of Cartman. This building was expensive and righteous. Annie was apparently wrong about the town not wanting change. Exhibit A, this building.

The lady at the front desk looked above the rim of her glasses and gave me a once over.

"Well you must be the new girl in town."

"Hi, I am Susanna Hightower, owner of Susanna's Flower Shop. I just wanted to stop in and introduce myself and bring you all a little something to say, 'Hi and Have a Beautiful Day!'"

"Well, aren't you a sweetheart?" The lady replied, and my heart fluttered. I was beginning to think this was a huge mistake from the way she looked at me when I walked in. "These are so adorable," she giggled with glee. "They will brighten up our day for certain."

Just then the tapping of high heels could be heard echoing down the hall, and the nice lady quickly sat back down behind her desk, timid and cowering like a dog that had been kicked too many times.

"Sara?" A very assertive voice called. "Do you have the city financials printed and copied yet for the meeting tonight?" She stopped mid-sentence and cocked her head to the side, glaring right through me as if she was sizing me up for a fight. I tensed up. Just as I was about to introduce myself— "Ms. Hightower, I presume?" Ms. Hightower? Who did she think I was? Did she know me?

"Yes, I am Susanna Hightower."

"Well, it is good to finally meet you." *Finally? Lady, I have been here a total of five minutes and you didn't make an effort to come to introduce yourself, so who the heck are you?* "I am Mayor Regina Gram." It was as if she read my mind, the way she said her name, as if I was supposed to bow and kiss her hand.

"Good to finally meet *you*," I replied with a bit of sarcasm. *Stop it, Susanna. You came to make friends not enemies, and especially not enemies with the Mayor of the town.*

"Well, Ms. Hightower, I assume that when you purchased the building from Ms. Markley, her current wedding bookings also transferred to you." What? What the hell was she talking about. Did I have weddings on the books? "I also am assuming you will be prepared for my son's wedding in two weeks," she continued. *Don't panic, Susanna. Don't panic. Fake it until you make it, smile, say something.*

"Ms. Gram—"

"Mayor Gram," she corrected me.

"Mayor Gram, I apologize for being so unprepared at the moment. I have not had a chance to go over the wedding bookings. When I return to the shop, I will make that a priority."

"I see. Well, not to overwhelm you, Ms. Hightower, but this will be the largest wedding this town has seen, and I expect nothing but perfection."

"Well then, your expectations will be exceeded, Mayor Gram. I am a perfectionist." *Please, Susanna, you can't even spell* perfectionist.

"Again, good to finally meet you." But before I could reply, just like a seasoned politician she cut me off and continued her conversation with Sara. "Sara, the reports. Are they or are they not ready?"

"Yes, ma'am. Ms. Hightower," the seemingly sweet Sara says, "is there anything else?"

"No, Sara. You have a beautiful day. I will be on my way." I smiled at Sara as if to say, "I'm sorry you work for the Devil, herself."

I didn't think anything could be worse than Annie telling me she shouldn't have sold me the business until I met the EVIL Regina Gram. Excuse me, the evil MAYOR Regina Gram. *Ms. Hightower…I will show her who Ms. Hightower is. She thinks she's intimidating? She has no idea who Ms. Hightower is.*

But first things first. I needed to find the paperwork for this upcoming wedding. After several stops introducing myself over and over again—sometimes with open arms and other times with a grimace and a sigh—I made my way to the feed store, a nervous feeling coming over me. K.C worked there.

I applied some fresh lipstick, shook off the bad Mayor juju, and walked in, searching the aisles for the man

of my dreams. Just then I saw him behind the counter,
reading the back of a label to an elderly gentleman in front
of me, explaining how much liquid to mix with water. *Look
at him, helping this man who apparently is having a hard
time reading the small print. He is gorgeous and
compassionate. Please marry me today.*

"Hey, you!" he says with the same charm as the day
before. "Didn't expect to have something so beautiful in the
feed store today." *Oh, be still my heart. He's talking about
the flowers, dummy, not you.*

"Well, a wise man told me I was going to bring
beauty to the town, so I wanted to prove him right. Is the
owner here? I just wanted to introduce myself to him as a
new fellow business owner in town."

"He's here."

"May I speak with him?"

"Sure."

"Can you get him, please?" *Man, K.C. may be cute, but he is not catching on too quick.*

"What? Do I not look like a business owner?"

"Ohhhh!" I laugh nervously and start to scratch my neck. *What a fool you are. You just insulted your future husband by thinking he was just the counter help.*

Just then I feel like I am on fire, and I can't stop scratching my neck. It's burning and itching. My throat is on fire! Is it humiliation or love? I'm not sure, but whatever it is hurts.

"Susanna? Are you ok? Your neck is breaking out. You must be allergic to something. Hopefully not flowers," he jokes. You have got to be kidding me! Could I be allergic to flowers? Wouldn't Mayor Gram love that! For me to die from flowers. Then she would have the final say.

I can't breathe and am beginning to hyperventilate. *What is wrong. Why is my neck on fire?*

"Susanna, come to the back. Let's get you a wet cloth. You can sit down in my office. Susanna, when you walked in did you walk down aisle three?"

"Ummm, maybe. I'm not sure. I saw you reading to the old man and didn't want to interrupt, so I might have leaned on the end counter."

"That's probably it. That's where we keep the weed killer. I bet you brushed into an open box and are having an allergic reaction to it. It's supposed to only kill weeds though, not beautiful flowers." If he only knew I was a weed. In the middle of a rose garden, I was the weed. The weed killer knew it.

~

I went home to the one room loft above Annie's garage that she rented to me for half of what she usually charged, with the agreement that I would clean her house every week. I reluctantly agreed, not sure I was cut out to clean Annie's house after spending an hour in her smoke-filled car, covered with the sweet, sweet smell of Vanilla Fields.

Her home was a bigger version of that four-door, baby blue sedan. Only, add two yapping chihuahuas who snapped at me when I walked in. I hadn't cleaned for Annie, yet she was kind enough to agree to let me have the next month to get settled in.

As I looked around the sad little loft and at the few boxes of all my possessions, I thought about the events of my day. The encounter with the mayor, my allergic reaction in front of K.C. I have always felt like a weed, like an unwanted thing growing amongst beauty. My mother was flawless. Her beauty was her greatest strength. She didn't even need grace and charm. All she had to do was smile at a man, and whatever she wanted he made sure she had.

My sister grew to be the same way, groomed to attract men to her and have them give in to her every wish. And when she was bored, she'd move on to the next. I guess my mother knew you couldn't have weeds in a garden of Eden, so she sent me to live with my Nana when I was fourteen. Awkward to the core, a weed, that was me. So, what was I doing again in a world of beautiful flowers?

Just as I was thinking about how I didn't fit in; the city hall building came to mind. It did not fit in at all. It was a rose among weeds, or so it seemed. It was glorious and clean and prestigious. This town was old and humble and content with its one stoplight and its brick roads.

Mayor Gram was like an extension of the building, or the building of her. She resembled the white marble floors and black granite countertops, with her perfectly altered, couture suit and her high heels with red soles. Those clothes were not bought at the 5 and Dime here in town, and her manicured fingers were not a priority that

was shared by the other women who lived here. Mayor
Gram could not be an original townsman. What was her
story?

Just then I popped out of bed in a panic. I forgot to
look for the wedding information for the upcoming
wedding of the Mayors son! I was so humiliated by my
allergic reaction that I started my pity party early and came
straight home. I knew I needed to find those papers, or I
was as good as gone. If I messed this up, I would get on a
plane and never look back. How hard could a few bouquets
and boutonnieres be to make?

Then next morning before the sun was even up, I
dressed as quickly as I could and practically ran to the
shop. I turned on my computer and the glow from the
screen illuminated my face. I freaked myself as the
shadows on the wall seemed to dance together to song only,
they could hear but I was determined to be prepared for
anything the Mayor might dish out and watched every

florist tips and tricks and how-to wedding flower videos I could find. They made making wedding arrangements seem simple enough. This would be a breeze. How big could the biggest wedding of this town possibly be? There were only seven hundred and two people in the town, and not all of them could be in the wedding party…right?

Now, I needed to find the contract and wedding information. I wanted to get made at Annie for being a horrible realtor and not telling me about any obligations I was under, but I am sure they were somewhere in fine print right under the sign here if you are an idiot with my signature so boldly written. I didn't have time for a self-pity. I started with the folders under the desk. I hadn't realized what a disorganized mess this place was. There was no rhyme or reason or any sort of filing system, just folders and papers with random orders on them. And abbreviations on notepads everywhere. Who knows what 1MCAA 8-22 means? I figured out that 8-22 must be the date, but was that this year or was it old? 8-22 was August 22nd, and that was in two weeks. Was this for the wedding? How was I to know?

I could not call the mayor. I would not cower before her like a timid dog that she liked to kick. I set the note aside in search of more information.

I had barely turned on my open sign and when the front door swung open so hard that the bell didn't even have time to ring. A tall, slender girl in yoga pants, drinking some kind of green mush, raced into the shop in complete panic mode. I'm such a chameleon and immediately take on her panic.

"Hi, can I help you?" I say in the calmest voice I can muster.

"Oh my gosh, are you Susanna?"

"Yes, I am. Can I help you?"

"I'm Katherine Wright Simmons. Geenie said you were here now."

"I'm sorry…Geenie?"

"Uh, Mayor Gram. She's my mother-in-law. Well, future mother-in-law. I am marrying Ian, her son. You can call me Kat. I have some changes—well, several changes—to my order. For one, I no longer love the thought of orchids. I mean, orchids in August? Eek. And I know it's last minute, but I really want jewel tones instead of pastels, and instead of one garland on the trees, I want two."

I blanked out somewhere after she said, "You can call me Kat." The only thought I had was *I wish the weed killer would have worked on me yesterday.*

"Susy? Susy? Are all these changes possible?"

"I… Katherine, I don't even know what the wedding order is," I say apologetically. "I'm sorry. I'm looking for a file or order form or something, but I haven't found anything yet."

"Oh, Sus, don't worry about it. I have it all right here in my binder." As she pulled out what appeared to big an old-school dictionary full of fabric samples and table layouts and cake pictures, she handed me this elaborate hand-drawn, to-scale picture of the most enchanting wedding I could ever imagine.

Huge trees—at least ten of them—with white lights. Tables with the biggest candelabras I have ever seen, with even more flowers arranged between the candles. An archway with thousands of flowers mingled with even more twinkling lights. Drawn underneath it, a bride and groom, and standing beside each one, a line of bridesmaids and groomsmen. I began to count, and after nine I started to panic as I realized this was a mock-up of the wedding, I said would exceed the mayor's expectations.

"Wow, is that fifteen attendants?"

"Oh yes, I didn't want to have our siblings in the wedding party, but Geenie insisted. Ian has 4 sisters, they're hideous, and now they're bridesmaids."

"Katherine, do you have the order form where Judith wrote down exactly what she was doing and…ummm…the cost?"

"Oh, she didn't write out an order form. She said just to tell her what flowers I wanted or send her a picture, and she would take care of it. Also, Judith was doing the wedding for us as a favor to the mayor. I don't really know why. Something about repaying her for something with the taxes or something. I really didn't listen. So, Susy, are the changes ok? No orchids, double garlands on the trees?" She chattered on, but all I heard was *free*.

Judith was going to do all of this for *free*? And I smarted off to the mayor when she asked if all the wedding bookings were also transferred, meaning I was stuck with this. Was I stuck with this? I was not under contract. I could not do this. How would I even pay for supplies? All I could do was stare at this overly caffeinated, Barbie doll of a human being.

"I…I…" I kept saying, stunned…

"Ok, well here is my cell, Susy patootie, and you just call if you have any questions. Also, the photographer is going to set up at eight that morning to take photos of you in action, documenting the whole day. So, make sure you look cute! I'll see ya, Susy Q!" As she left out the door with the same gusto she blew in with.

What the hell was that whirlwind? Geenie…she called the mayor "Geenie." Susy Q? As I sat there baffled, the phone rang.

"Hello? Flower Shop," I answered, too afraid to even answer and it was all I could do to even remember my name, much more announce it.

"Yes, I need a dozen red roses sent to city hall, to Sara, and please just sign the card 'Wink Wink,'" said a very distinguished-sounding man. *Oh, good for Sara!* I was happy at the thought that I was getting to see Sara smile again, today.

After the man on the other end read off his card numbers, he said, "Now, you do know you are not allowed to tell anyone who these came from, not even Sara if she asks? She won't, but it's confidential." *Is there a code,* I thought, a sort of HIPAA code that florists are supposed to abide by? And then he told me the name of the cardholder. Richard Gram.

GRAM? As in Regina Gram, the mayor? Maybe Richard is her brother-in-law and Sara is his girlfriend. Oh my, could he be the mayor's husband? Was the mayor's husband sending flowers to another woman? And not just any flowers, but a dozen red, romantic roses to Sara, the mayor's secretary? Sara's soft look yesterday may not have been timid at all, but more a look of guilt. Like a dog who just got caught chewing its owner's favorite shoe, or a woman who was sleeping with the mayor's husband.

"Um, yes sir, completely confidential. I will have these delivered in about an hour."

I don't know why I felt any sort of empathy to the cold-hearted mayor, but I felt like I was betraying her by delivering flowers to Sara from her husband. I walked the arrangement in, and Sara smiled as if she knew already, they were for her. Then she got the same timid look and wouldn't look me in the eye as I placed them on her desk and said, "This delivery is for you." She knew I knew, and it was more than awkward.

"Ms. Hightower!" The sound of my last name screeching out of her mouth was like nails on a chalkboard. "Ms. Hightower, can you please come to my office?" beckons the mayor. *What if she asks about the roses? What if she confronts me and blames me for the affair her husband and secretary are having?* I walked into her office like a child walking into the principal's office.

"Ms. Hightower, Katherine tells me she met with you earlier and she has made some changes, yet again, for the wedding. My future daughter-in-law is no longer allowed to make changes without my approval to the order. While I agree that orchids in August are tacky, I told her that the first time she made the order, so I approve of nixing all orchids. However, I do not see any reason to add another garland of flowers to already magnificent trees." The mayor did not seem to have the same affection towards Kat as Kat did her.

"Also, I have decided that I want Richard, that's my husband,"—*Yes,* I thought to myself. *Richard, your husband, not your brother-in-law*— "to walk me down the aisle as a sign of our love and commitment to each other and as an example of what a successful marriage should look like. Katherine's parents are divorced." She said the word "divorced" with such condemnation, it was as if Katherine's parents sold children into slavery for money. "My son has chosen to marry out of his league, and I do not mean he is marrying up. But I will not bore you with my son's poor choices. I just wanted us to be on the same page as to who is allowed to make changes from here on out."

Again, my face was bewildered. It's like I was in a beehive, the queens fighting for the throne, but I was the only one about to get stung.

"Crystal clear, Mayor. No more changes. While we are discussing the wedding flowers, Kat…Katherine mentioned that Judith was doing the flowers as payment for something."

"Yes, Judith owed several thousands of dollars in back taxes to the city. I took care of them for her. So, therefore, the new owner of the business does not have to pay them either. The trade of florals for the wedding should still be warranted." *Dear Lord, she's intimating.*

"Yes ma'am, understood." *Why am I letting her kick me?* Empathy regarding her cheating husband and the scandalous secretary had me weak. Even after she spoke so detesting of her future daughter-in-law and her family.

"Good then, Ms. Hightower. Have a nice afternoon." And just like that, I was dismissed.

~

"Hey, flower lady," I hear as I walk out of the city hall. "You hungry?" *Oh, my heart, it's K.C.* He was walking toward me.

"Hi!"

"I'm headed to the café for some lunch. It's greasy and way overpriced, but I'm buying if you want to join me." How could I say no to that smile? Could anyone say no to that smile? I bet he had never heard the word "No" uttered from a female, ever.

"You know what? I am starving. It has been a crazy busy morning, and I think grease is precisely what my chaotic mind needs right now."

We sat down in the corner booth, and a waitress who couldn't have been more than seventeen and very, very pregnant took our order. She blushed when K.C. asked if the apple pie was anywhere near as sweet as she was. *Dear God, he is a flirt*, but in a charming, natural way. He wasn't forcing cheesy lines. He effortlessly delivered words that made women weak in the knees. I rolled my eyes, trying to play the feminist card.

"Really? She's about to pop, and you're flirting with her?"

He laughed. "I'm not flirting. She looks like it has been a long time since someone's said something nice to her. I'm trying to brighten her day." *Oh, he is smooth. It's God-given talent, the charm in him.* "Well I know the new florist in town who can hook you up with some flowers that can brighten her day if you want." *Then I remembered the arrangement he ordered the other day, and realized I was having lunch with someone's husband or boyfriend, I wasn't Sara. He was beautiful and genuine, but we shouldn't be eating lunch together, as I begin to feel uncomfortable K.C charmed in with his smile and the way he looked into my eyes I couldn't help but feel like he could make my day better.*

"So, tell me, Susanna, why has your day been so crazy busy in such an easy-going town?"

"Well, I…it just takes some time, trying to figure out the back end of things at the shop."

"Anything I can help you with? I've owned the feed store almost ten years now."

"Well, you can find all the orders," I said, laughing. "Judith didn't have much of a filing system. I should have known when she did not have any P&Ls."

"You bought a business without any profit and loss statements? Ok well my first advice would be to NEVER do that again"

"Ha! Thanks! Have you ever thought of changing your name to Captain Obvious, and Yes "I replied sheepishly "I bought a business I knew nothing about in a town, I know nothing about, and I sit here having lunch with someone who knows nothing about me."

"Huh." He said as he leans back in the booth as if his body said, "I know everything about you Susanna, but his words were "You must have wanted to desperately leave New York."

"You could say that." I stared blankly into his intense brown eyes as the word "desperately" echoed in my thoughts. *Dear K.C., if you only knew how* desperately *I am trying not to be a weed in a world full of flowers.*

~

I walked back to the shop after lunch, still aching over the words K.C. had left me with. "You must have wanted desperately to escape New York." Was it New York I trying to escape? Was it Ethan and his obsessive need to make sure it was known that I would never be his equal?

I was trying to shake off that haunting feeling when the cowbell made its *clang clang* noise, and a customer walked in.

"Hi! How can I help you?"

"Are you the new owner?" an elderly, but not fragile, lady said.

"Yes ma'am." *Ma'am…I am really getting this Texan thing down, with all my Yes ma'ams and No sirs.* "I am Susanna Hightower. Is there something I can help you with?"

I am Judith Markley, formerly of Judith's Petal Patch. This was my business before you moved to town," she said with a sarcastic undertone, as if I were the cause of her business's demise.

"Well, it is nice to meet you, Ms. Markley. I can't get over what a fantastic building this is. The walls have fascinating stories behind them, I can feel it. If only they could talk."

"Oh, dear, you should know the walls aren't the only ones who keep secrets. You will find out soon that it is in your best interest to also keep your mouth shut. What happens here, as they say, stays here." I cocked my head in confusion, yet it was crystal clear what she was telling me. What I didn't understand is why she was telling me.

I gathered my composure and again asked if there was anything, I could do for her.

"Yes, Susanna, I would like to send some flowers to my husband." Her husband? Didn't Annie tell me her husband passed away? In response to the look on my face, she replied in the same, snide manner as before. "To the cemetery. Are you offering that service here, or is that a thing only small-town business owners do? Not big city event florists such as yourself."

Geez, do all these people talk in code? Big city event florist? I mean, if you counted the one arrangement, I did for Mr. Wonderfuls special lady and the eight free arrangements I took to the business owners, along with the red roses that burned a scarlet "A" in my chest, you might have called me a florist, but big events? Far from it…. *Oh, there is the biggest wedding this town has ever seen. The one that, because of your mishandling and my naivety, has led to me digging myself further into this hole of debt I've found myself in, due to purchasing a business and a building that's biggest asset is "the oldest chandelier in the county." If that's your idea of big event, Ms. Markley, then believe what you want.*

"Yes ma'am, I am a full-service florist, and I can deliver a beautiful arrangement to Mr. Markley. What did you have in mind?"

"Well, his birthday is in two weeks, and I would like an arrangement on an easel in the shape of a football, with a ribbon that says, 'State Champion Forever.' I want it fresh and delivered on Saturday, August 20th, by 8:00 A.M." My only thought was, *Why so specific a time?* Was he going somewhere?

"Yes ma'am, I can have that ready by then. Which cemetery is he at?"

"Ha! Oh, Susanna, what a funny girl you are! Silly, there is only one cemetery here. You forget you're in a small town now. One cemetery, one funeral home, one stoplight, one church. You, my dear, are literally in a one-horse town. Welcome!" Her lips said "Welcome," but the way she said it was not welcoming at all. It was more like "Welcome to the last day of life as you know it. Prepare for the end."

I channeled my inner shark tank, business persona, and, with all the confidence I could muster, asked if she wanted to pay in cash or credit card. She stared at me like I was a bug to be crushed.

"Just bill me, 'k hun?"

"Absolutely, Ms. Markley. Where should I send the bill?"

"Oh, Annie has all my info. Get it from her. I am late for the chamber of commerce meeting, so I must run. Ta Ta!" And just like that, she was gone as if she were never even here. People in this town are outstanding about ending the conversation before you have a chance to state your side.

Wait! Did she say chamber of commerce meeting? Why was she still attending those, and why was I not? However, I couldn't handle another run-in with the mayor that day, so I chose to look at it as a blessing in disguise that I was not there.

I took out my notepad and wrote the order for the easel of fresh flowers in the shape of a football, with the ribbon to read, "State Champion Forever." I wondered what the meaning behind that was. State champion? I vaguely remembered overhearing some men in the café talking about "going to state" this year and a stacked team. It didn't seem like the kind of conversation I felt would have significance on my day, so I didn't pay attention. I partly wished that I would have.

As I finished writing the order, I tried to estimate my cost and how much to charge Ms. Markley. Would she pay? Would Annie give me grief when I asked her for Judith's info so that I could bill her? Judith was such a great friend to Annie that Annie didn't charge her a commission, and she sold me a business she knew was destined to fail but did so out of her loyalty to her friend.

Oy! I had a feeling this would be, yet another arrangement Ms. Judith Markley made me eat.

I looked down at the date. August 20th at 8:00 A.M. The mayor's son's wedding and photography started at 8:00 A.M! That bitch! SHE KNEW THE DATE AND TIME OF THE WEDDING! Another setup, another reason to cause me to fail.

No way! Nope, Ms. Markley, I am not going to let you have the upper hand. I will bill you, and I don't care who it bothers! I will deliver your State Champion Forever easel, and I will be a big city event florist for the biggest wedding this town has ever seen. And you know what? I will do it without getting paid. And if it causes me to go under, I will do it with all the gusto of a biggest city girl this small town has ever seen!"

For the first time since arriving, I was ready to show this small town what I was made of. I went to the back and started organizing the orders I could make out. I started

calling all the numbers and confirming everything.

Surprisingly, the more people I talked to, the more people

were friendly to me, genuinely welcoming. I would no

longer be afraid of not being liked. I had a business to run.

~

"Hey, Annie, how are you this evening?" I asked as I

walked into the backyard to my apartment over the garage.

Annie was there, working in her garden, wearing a pair of

what appeared to be men's overalls. The tall, skinny,

washed-out redhead looked like something out of the

Farmers' Almanac. Her skin, weathered by the sun and

wrinkled even more from the chain smoking, somehow fit

her personality.

She looked shocked when I asked her how she was,

but in true Annie fashion, she replied, "Well, the only way I

would be better is if I were six feet under with a rock over my head that read 'Here Lies Annie, she is better now!'" I

had to chuckle. I wasn't sure if she was serious or if that

was just her humor. Either way, I was determined to no

longer be intimated by the townspeople of Cartman, Texas.

"Sounds good, Annie. Oh, and, Annie, try and have

a nice night. I will be by in the morning to clean if that's

ok. I know we agreed I didn't have to start yet, but you

have done so much, I want to say thanks."

"Oh, you know what, Susanna? Tomorrow is not

good. I have some showings in the morning, and then my

daddy is coming for lunch. I am a daddy's girl, Susanna.

Every Saturday, like clockwork, we have our weekly lunch.

I am hoping these squashes aren't too ripe to fry up.

Susanna, have you ever had fried squash 'fore? Oh

goodness, it is yummy." Annie seems to drift off to another

time. "Yes, I learned to fry squash from my great-

grandmother, right there in that kitchen. Sundays we would

have a roast and new potatoes, along with fried squash,

cucumber salad, sweet tea, and for dessert, peaches and cottage cheese."

Annie had a smile on her face as she recalled the past, yet her smile was sad, as if the memory of that meal hurt her heart for some reason. She shook it off and was back to Annie.

"Anyhow, that was a long time ago. Things have changed since then, but my daddy and I still have lunch. G'night, Susanna. I will holler atchya later." And in true Cartman fashion, Annie was gone before I could reply.

Something about that conversation made me miss home. Not New York, but Livingston, Montana. My home, my small town, my past. These people only thought I was big city, but the truth of it is I was smaller than this town could ever imagine. Take me out of my knock-off brand name clothes, and I am a thrift store girl who grew up behind a bingo hall in a two-bedroom mobile home, with a mother who sometimes made an appearance and a sister who hated the very sight of me. Except for my Nana who loved me dearly I could not wait to leave that life behind.

Out of nowhere I had the sudden urge to run away from the present, to leave the image of a big city girl and go back to the life in the two-bedroom mobile home where I felt safe, if only for a moment.

I went upstairs to my one-bedroom loft, with rickety wooden floors and a twin bed pushed against the wall, with a quilt that had a red star in the middle. It was so old you could almost see through it, but it was as soft as the most exquisite silks you could buy. My nana sat every night for a year in her green, velvet rocking chair, hand sewing the pieces of cloth together. I can close my eyes and see her rocking and sewing, the whole time listening to the news and shaking her head in disbelief at the headline stories. She never had to say a word out loud, but I knew with every nod and shake of her head she was talkin to Jesus.

She gave me that quilt the day I told her I was miserable living there and I was better than living behind a bingo hall in a trailer house. The thought that I hurt her that day still leaves me empty. The idea that I can never take back those words still haunts me. The quilt is all I have left of her, the quilt and now the flower shop that I bought with the money she left to me. It was even more motivation not to fail her…again and I cried myself to sleep that night missing my Nana.

~

I woke up a little later than usual. I guess the trip down Annie's and my memory lanes took a lot out of me, mentally. I felt refreshed, though, for the first time in ages. I felt as if I was relaxed. I didn't feel like Chicken Little, waiting for the sky to fall.

I decided I would head to the shop and make Annie an arrangement for her lunch with her daddy. I had a fresh order of daisies in the cooler and some red gingham ribbon that seemed like the perfect match to peaches and cottage cheese.

I got dressed and made my way down the main street of town. When I got near my building, a muscular, blond young man was looking in my window. He did not seem to be lost, yet he did not appear to be from here.

"Hi!" I yelled. "I am almost there, give me just a minute." As I started to jog, not wanting my customer to leave, it happened. My flip-flop flipped right out from under me, and I flopped right down on the sidewalk, face first. It was like even the sidewalk in this town hated me. I wanted to cry from the stinging of my cut knees and elbows. I wanted to cry harder from the sheer embarrassment of faceplanting in front of who seemed to be a prestigious person.

"Hi. Susanna, is it?"

"Yes, sadly I am Susanna," I said. At that point, who would have been proud to be me?

I unlocked the door. As the gentleman followed behind, I couldn't even find the energy to ask if I could help him.

He followed me to the front counter and said, "Hi, Susanna. I am Ian Gram, Kat's fiancé. Or, as most people around here refer to me, Mayor Gram's son. I wanted to come in and order some flowers for Kat and my mother. Unfortunately, karma cursed me with both their birthdays on the same day." He chuckled.

I smiled in relief. Ian Gram, the mayor's son, was nothing like his mother. He was polite and charming and had a genuine smile, and when he referred to himself as Kat's fiancé, his eyes lit up like that was the best thing to ever happen to him.

"I would like eleven fresh red roses and one silk red rose arranged together for Kat, and I want the card to read 'Dearest Kat, you are the greatest thing to ever happen to me. When you laugh, my world stops. When you cry, my heart drowns. I don't know what I did for you to ever want me in your life. All I know is I will love you until the last rose dies. Forever yours, Ian.'"

I couldn't imagine being loved by a man so deeply. I wrote the card with a smile and hope—hope that there was someone out there who could love me like that.

"And for my mother, just throw together whatever you have on hand. Nothing extravagant and no roses. And I want the card to read 'Hope you have a Happy Birthday. I am sorry I am such a son of a bitch'" He did not laugh or break face. He was stone-cold and angry. I didn't know how to respond. Two different attitudes for two very different women in his life. It was clear who he was choosing. The mayor may have had the final say in the wedding flowers, but from the sound of it, she had no say in the marriage.

"Can you deliver those today after lunch sometime? Here is my mother's address, and here is where Kat is staying. They'll both be home after lunch. This morning they are finalizing the menu. Say a prayer for the caterer, Susanna." He laughed.

"The caterer? How about the florist?" I replied without thinking. He laughed even harder.

"Susanna, please don't let my mother intimidate you with all the 'this is the biggest wedding this town has ever seen' nonsense. Kat and I just want a beautiful day, and if that means we have sunflowers in mason jars or those little white flowers, baby's butt—"

I grinned. "Baby's Breath, you mean."

"Susanna, what I mean is that all we want is to say, 'I do' and begin our life together as man and wife. The flowers are an added bonus. Our love is what will make the day beautiful, no matter what my mother says. Kat sometimes gets caught up in the competition of trying to outdo her, but she honestly feels the same way. So please don't stress. I know it will be beautiful. My uncle told me you bring a lot of beauty to this town."

I swallowed hard, like so hard I almost choked. *Did he just say "Uncle"? Is K.C., the feed store owner, the mayor's...BROTHER? Oh, sweet baby Jesus, shoot me now. How can I marry the brother to the devil herself? Although, I do see now where Ian gets his charm and swag. Those genes run deep.*

"Oh, how sweet of your uncle to say that! I appreciate any compliment I can get. Thanks, Ian, for your kind words about the wedding, but I am genuinely going to do my best to make your day the fairytale you and Kat deserve." *Even with the wicked witch attending. Maybe a house will fall on her and her red-bottomed shoes before then*. "I will have these delivered after lunch."

I couldn't help but giggle while writing out the card to the mayor from her son, but then the empathic feeling washed over me again, the guilt for delivering flowers from her cheating, no-good husband to her backstabbing secretary resurfacing. And now I had to deliver flowers to her on her birthday that iterated the fact that she is total B.

I also couldn't stop thinking about the fact that K.C. was the mayor's brother. Perhaps I was mistaken. Probably, K.C. is Ian's dad's brother. I would think having a wife and girlfriend would require those same flirtatious genes that K.C. and Ian possessed. That was it! K.C. had to be Richard's brother. K.C. and Richard…that made sense.

I focus back to the task at hand and make the arrangements for Kat and the mayor. Then I make the arrangement of daisies for Annie.

As I am leaving to deliver the flowers to Annie's house, I see the Mayor and Kat walking out of the bank together, the mayor with a look of victory, and poor Kat with a look of defeat. I couldn't help but wonder what was going on. They were supposed to be at the caterer. The mayor caught me staring in confusion at them. With one cold look, she made it very clear that this was none of my business. The look said, "Tell anyone you saw me here, I will end you." It is crazy how someone so powerful can stop a person in their tracks with just a straightforward look.

I, again, in a moment of weakness cowered down to the mayor's intimidation and replied with a look that said "Understood." Why did I keep letting my empathetic waves of emotion for that callused lady get to me?

I decided to head back to the shop instead of to Annie's. I didn't think I could take her dry sarcasm today, not after that run-in with the mayor, and not before I had to deliver flowers to her. I dreaded the mayor's discovery of the fact that I knew how tense the relationship with her son was."

I watched the clock for the rest of the morning with a nauseous ache in my stomach, waiting for delivery time. Maybe I could call Ian and tell him I ran out of flowers for his mother's arrangement and avoid the situation altogether. He was so lovely to me, though, and calmed all my stresses about the wedding. *He is my ally, and these days I need all the partners I can get.*

At one o'clock I decided to head to the mayor's home. I went all the way down main street, almost out of town, and turned left onto one of the only new roads in the town. The homes were historic but in pristine condition, the yards were manicured flawlessly, and there was a wreath on every single door on every single house on the street.

There were only a few houses—six, maybe—and the road actually turned into a cul-de-sac, with the most significant house sitting at the end.

It was white with black shutters and a red front door. The magnolia tree in the front yard seemed as stoic as any statue representing a past president. It was noble, and the heritage that it represented ran as deep as its roots. The American flag hanging on the front porch blew perfectly in the wind. The mat by the front door said "WELCOME," and handprints of five young children in the sidewalk made it seem like I just stepped into a Hallmark movie starring the perfect, beautiful family with their adopted golden retriever.

I rang the doorbell and, for a split second, contemplated a ring and run. As I was preparing to set the flowers down by the door, it opened, and there, with all the grace and charm of a southern lady, was the mayor.

She was a beautiful woman with blonde hair that had the just-blown out look every time you saw her, crystal clear blue eyes, perfect makeup that enhanced her high cheekbones, and heart-shaped lips with just the right amount of red lipstick. She was dressed in a simple black dress with a large diamond pendant adorning her neck. I never realized how graceful the mayor actually was, but standing in the doorway of her picture-perfect home, the mayor radiated.

She smiled when she saw me with the flowers, and in girl-like excitement she squealed, "OH, FOR ME?" I wanted to die. I wanted to take them away and say I had the wrong address. She was excited to be getting flowers on her birthday just like any typical girl would be, and I was about to crush that excitement with a very unkind card from her son. There it was again. How could I feel for this woman while at the same time loathing everything about how she acted?

She quickly snatched the vase out of my hands, and with much excitement opened the card. Her face trembled for a brief second, but with the biggest smile and a fake laugh, she turned without saying a word and walked back into her glorious home as if nothing was wrong. Through the window on the porch, I saw her place the flowers on the center of the table, proudly displaying them, card still attached. Perhaps I mistakenly took the message. Maybe this was some inside joke only a mother and son would understand. Did I have it all wrong?

~

I followed the directions that Ian wrote out for me as to where to deliver Kat's flowers. It was almost five miles out of town, and I am thankful I had the courage to ask Annie to borrow her four-door, baby blue sedan but I was afraid that by the time I arrived at Kat's the roses would no longer have the fresh aroma only a red rose can produce, and smell more like a day-old ashtray.

I pulled into Cartman Mobile Home Estates and found lot number 42. I've always found it fascinating the way mobile home parks always add the word "estate" to their title, as if some socialite were to drive by and say "Oh, I hope to have a home in the Meadowbrook Mobile Home Estates someday."

As I pulled up to the tiny home that could be moved in the blink of an eye, I flashed back to the one I grew up in, as it was a cookie cutter version of the beige tin box with brown window trim. The front steps barely qualified as safe, and when the front door opened, if I didn't step down, I would be knocked off as the door opened to the outside. Only someone who knows "estate" living would know to step down off of the three-wooden-stepped "front porch."

I knocked, and Kat immediately opened the door. Her face was red, and her eyes were swollen. Her mascara had run so much it stained her face. She tried to hide the fact that she looked as if her best friend just moved away.

"Hey Kat! I have a special delivery for you on your birthday!"

"I don't want them, Susanna. Take them back, please," she said with an emptiness.

I was shocked and confused. "Katherine, are you okay? These were sent with a special message in the card. Here, take them, read the card."

Katherine took the card and smiled as she read the loving words Ian had written her. Through a smile she burst into tears, and just like a child who can't catch their breath she said, "Take these back, Susanna. I don't want them. I am calling off the wedding. I am leaving Ian. I am not in love with him."

I heard her say that she was leaving and was not in love, but I knew firsthand what not being in love and leaving looked like, and Katherine looked more in love at this moment than the day she walked into my flower shop.

"Katherine," I say as calmly as possible.

"Susanna. You have no idea what it is like living here in Cartman, Texas. They should really consider changing the name to Crazy Town, Texas. I feel as if it is suffocating me, and each day I stay here I lose a little more of myself. I was marrying Ian for all the wrong reasons. He was my ticket out of here, and now that he is being groomed to take over, I just don't think I want to be married anymore. Not to him and defiantly not to this town."

I could not believe what Katherine was saying. How could a woman fake loving a man so much that he becomes so head over heels in love with her that he can't wait to be married to her? I refused to believe that this love was not real. I refused because it was the only hope I had for finding someone to love me until my last rose died. I was not going to let the relationship be broken by Crazy Town.

"Katherine, I will leave the flowers here on the steps. I made a promise to deliver them. You don't have to take them inside, but can I please just say something?" She looked at me with a plea for help, and just like the look the mayor shot me earlier, I knew she was begging for me to say I understood.

"Katherine, I have been here in this town a very short time, and in that time, I have witnessed only a little crazy, mixed with a whole lot of kind." I wanted to add in some scandal, but I kept it to myself. "Today a man walked—no, he floated—on clouds into my shop and introduced himself to me as Kat's fiancé. He said it the way the president of the United States proclaims his title in his speeches, and then he told me that the flowers that would be at your wedding would only be added beauty because the real beauty of the day would be your marriage.

"Katherine…Kat, I have never been in love or known love like that from a man. And if I did, I would not let the CRAZY of the town keep me from him. This world is big, much more significant than Cartman, Texas, and finding that kind of love may not happen twice. Please think about what I am telling you before you leave. If tomorrow you feel the same way, then call me, and I will buy your bus ticket because I know what it's like to feel suffocated and desperately want to escape. Happy Birthday, Katherine!"

~

What a day, and it was only mid-afternoon. I got back to the shop, and there was a message on my machine.

"Hey Suse! It's K.C." Just hearing his voice on the machine sent goosebumps up and down my arms. *Maybe he's calling to confess his undying love for me and how he knew it the minute we locked eyes.*

"Hey Suse, I need to order some flowers again. Not roses, but something special. This lady has my heart and I need to cheer her up today." *Why do I want to spit in this poor girl's eye?* It wasn't like she'd stolen him from me. They were probably the perfect couple who kissed every time they said hello and goodbye, and who shared a drink at the movie while holding hands and laughing at all the same dumb parts, as if they were not two but one single person.

"I will be by around four o'clock to pick them up, if that works. If not, give me a call here at the feed store. Thanks, Suse. See ya later."

Most of the time I find it more than annoying when people refer to me as anything other than Susanna. But whenever K.C. called me Suse, or Susy, or anything that meant he was talking to me, I wanted to call my momma, Ethan, and my tenth-grade history teacher who called me out in class saying I would never amount to anything because I couldn't recite the Pythagorean theorem, and tell them that Oh, Susanna has finally made something of herself. She has found someone who believes in her and doesn't say "Oh, Susanna" in a condescending way, but in an endearing, heartfelt way.

But I hadn't found that yet. I had found a man who was so good with words he had no idea that his simple "Hello" made my heart beat out of my chest. That his innocent flirtation made me want to have his children. That the thought of his sending flowers to a woman he was obviously smitten with made me want to run back to New York and live a lonely, empty life with Ethan, rather than to think about him being in love with someone that wasn't me.

As the clock neared four, I had the flower arrangement ready. It was the perfect combination of coral peonies and blue anemones and a few yellow daisies for the cheerful element in the arrangement.

I was down and out and didn't know if I could even find the energy to be happy when K.C. walked in. After the run-in on the street with the mayor and Kat, and then the face to face with Cruella Deville, and Kat's emotional breakdown, the empath in me could not handle any more human interaction. My energy was depleted, and all I wanted to do was go crawl in my bed and wrap myself in my quilt from Nana, close my eyes, pretend it was her arms, and try as hard as I could to hear her voice telling me, "Susanna, sweetheart, have you ever noticed that even on a rainy day the sun still shines? You just may not be able to see it through the clouds. It's all in your perception. The sun still shines no matter how many clouds in the sky."

My nana was always older than she was. Her hard life as a child, growing up on the Indian reservation, and then raising my mom by herself after my grandfather abandoned her showed in every wrinkle on her face. She was wise though, wise beyond imagination. And like me, she felt every emotion of those around her.

I was tired and on the verge of crying when K.C. walked in the door.

"Susanna Hightower, how are you doing today?"

I smiled and replied, "Fine."

He stopped and was serious for the first time since we'd met. "Susanna, are you okay? You look like you are about to…" That was the last thing I heard before I woke up in the hospital.

~

"Susanna? Susie Patootie? Hey lady, wake up! You gave us a scare."

Through my squinting eyes I could make out a woman, and the more she talked I knew the familiar voice. It was Kat and standing beside her was Ian. Why were

Katherine and Ian standing over me in a hospital? What happened?

"Susy Q, you passed out and gashed your head on your counter. You have some stitches and took quite the snooze, but the doctors have been running tests and cannot find anything wrong with you."

"I…I don't remember anything after delivering your flowers, Kat."

She abruptly interrupted me, "Yes, you told me you weren't feeling well, and I said you made the most beautiful bouquet of red roses I had ever seen, and Ian shouldn't have, but I know what a romantic guy my Ian is, so I didn't expect anything less."

I smiled at her as she squeezed my hand and mouthed "Thank you" while Ian was texting.

"Uncle K.C said he will be by later to take you home. He had something to tend to this morning. You gave him a mild heart attack, I think. He has been known to stop a few ladies' hearts with his smile, but he thought it had literally happened this time." Ian chuckled.

I didn't find it funny. I found it arrogant, K.C. thinking he literally stopped my heart.

"Susy Q, we are going to head out now that you are awake. We have to go finalize the cakes—eeekk! I cannot believe the wedding will be over by this time next week!"

If my head wasn't already about to pop off my neck, I think hearing those words would have caused a total explosion.

Kat and Ian left, and as the door closed behind them, I could see something on the table next to me. They were flowers but not the flowers from my cooler, so I assumed Kat and Ian brought them. Since the hospital was in the nearest city to Cartman, I supposed they'd stopped in the gift shop.

It was kind of nice having someone send me flowers. I never thought when I bought the shop that I would probably never have anyone send me flowers ever again. Not that it happened too often before, but I did have a secret admirer in junior high who sent me a red carnation to school. I later found out it was the class nerd, but still the flower made my day.

I got out of bed and felt like my legs were concreted down. It was an odd feeling, and the throbbing headache made even the slightest light hitting my eyes feel like razors cutting my corneas. But I was excited to read what the card said.

As I opened it and started to read, I had the same shiver that went down my spine the very first day I stepped into my new building froze me solid. "Oh Susanna, oh don't you lie to me. You knew when you left me this would end up bad-a-lee. Hope you didn't embarrass yourself in front of Prince Charming. See you soon! E."

How did he know where I was? How did he know K.C was with me, and what made him think he was Prince Charming? I felt the world go black again.

As I was coming to, a doctor was standing in my room.

"Susanna Hightower. I am Dr. Evans. I have a few questions for you if you feel up to answering."

"Why does my head—" I started but couldn't get the words out before I felt as if I were going to throw up. I felt like I had too much champagne, only I hadn't had one ounce of alcohol in ages.

"Susanna, from what we can tell you are suffering from a severe migraine. Have you or anyone in your family ever battled migraines before?"

A migraine, why didn't I think of it? Maybe because I thought every time my mother was laid up for days on end in her bedroom, crying that her head hurt and puking her guts out, getting fired from job after job because she missed so many days, that it was nothing more than a hangover caused by a weekend of boozing with random men. She was sick, she was in pain, and I was horrible. And now karma was having her revenge.

"My mother. My mother suffered from migraines, but this is my first episode with one."

He went over all the possible triggers and warning signs, and prescribed migraine medication. Just as he was finishing up by telling me to relax and to try not to let little things stress me out, K.C. walked in the door holding a bouquet of balloons.

Balloons? That's what you take a child who just had their tonsils removed. Nothing says "we are just friends" more than balloons.

"Hi, K.C. Thanks for picking me up."

"Hey Suse, no problem. After all, you forgot to charge me for my last order. You know, after you banged your head into the counter and all." He grinned but it was forced. You could feel an awkward tension now. He didn't seem as smooth as before.

The ride home was silent mostly because I was trying my hardest to concentrate on anything other than the fact that the motion and bumpy ride in his four-wheeled drive truck made me want to start throwing up.

I told him I was living behind Annie Deets's house, and he said, "Yea, I know where that is." And those were the last words K.C. and I said until he pulled into the drive. I tried to get out a "Thanks," but before I could get a chance he said, "Take care of yourself, Susanna."

He didn't offer to walk me up or tuck me in or sit with me through the night. Nope. Just like my grandfather, my father, and every other man that came into my life, when the tough times arrived, they were gone like they were never there in the first place. K.C. wasn't any different, but my heart wasn't ready to accept that fact.

~

I took my migraine medicine along with some sleep aid, and I was in such a deep sleep that when I finally realized the pounding on my door was not my head, my whole body tensed up, startled. I leapt out of bed and to the window without really knowing what I was doing, but I had a scared feeling.

Just as I'd started to pull the curtain, "Susanna, open the door, sweetheart. It's me."

There he was in all his New York glory, standing on my balcony. Ethan had the looks of a spoiled frat boy: dirty blond hair that was perfectly shaggy, a pink polo shirt rolled three quarters up his forearm, and khaki shorts and deck shoes. He stuck out like a sore thumb here in Cartman.

"I am sick, Ethan. Go away."

Just then the door opened, and Ethan walked in.

"My…. Aren't we trusting of our small-town neighbors? You know most serial killers live in a small town just like this? In fact, I think I read once somewhere that Texas has the most serial killers on record."

I looked at him like he was an idiot but couldn't help but laugh at him. As immature and degrading as Ethan could be, he had a way of making me laugh. That was what I first fell for in him. That, and he promised me the world the first night we met.

He was in Livingston closing a deal on a power plant, and I was a bartender at the local bar and grill. He said all the right things. The very next day, without a thought I was on a plane to New York, desperately escaping my life in Livingston. And three years later I was on a flight, desperately avoiding my life in New York. Maybe I was more like the men in my life than I realized.

~

Ethan somehow managed his way into staying with me for the day. Maybe it was that I was still afraid of passing out again and no one finding me, or maybe it was because in spite of all his bad ways I still felt safe with Ethan.

We spent the entire day watching comedy movies and laughing at all the same parts that most people find beneath their intellectual level. But it was when he reached over and took a sip of my soda and for a moment I wanted to say "Take me home Ethan. I'm sorry. I made a mistake coming here. I really do love you."

Just at the time I was about to open my mouth, Ethan answered his phone, and he went from a man who was taking care of the love of his life to the spoiled frat boy. I heard him say, "Dude, that sounds epic, but I'm in Texas. Seems ole Susanna got overheated, either from the Texas sun or some dirty old cowboy. Either way I am here to iterate to her that she's a fool and she can't make it without me. But don't drink all the whiskey, dude. It's on when I get back."

I felt like vomiting again. Not from the migraine but because I was almost fooled into falling for Ethan again.

"Alright, Ethan, thanks for coming. Time to leave. But wait, how did you know?"

"Where you were? I have my ways, Susanna. It wasn't that hard. The girl at the bank told me where she wired the money. I was about to walk into your shop when I saw you talking to that old cowboy. He was looking at you like you were the prettiest flower in the place. I got jealous, and just as I was about to come in and break his nose you nose-dived into your counter. I followed the ambulance to the hospital.

"Susanna, I really do miss you. I was coming to tell you that my life is empty without you in it. Please come back with me, baby. I only say those things to the guys, so I don't get jabbed at for being a schmuck in love. I am in love."

Why is he saying all the right things when I am so weak? Be strong, I told myself over and over.

"Ethan, the words you say are the things I want to hear. But when I left, I made a vow that I was not going to quit myself this time."

He looked like a little boy standing there, and I thought I almost saw a tear in his eye.

"Susanna, is this about that dirty cowboy?" The way he kept referring to K.C. as a dirty cowboy had my blood boiling. "I can't believe you are choosing someone who prefers to spend his day in horse poop rather than coming home with me to New York."

Ethan was showing his true colors, all the shades of red when he loses or thinks he has lost. Everything in Ethan's life was about competition and winning, and I was no different than the rugby trophies in his room. I was a trophy. It wasn't me he loved.... It was the thought of being able to beat me that he was in love with.

He started stomping and throwing a fit and spewing words about K.C. as if K.C. and I were an actual couple, though I had yet to try and convince him we weren't. I guess I enjoyed the fact that he thought another man could want poor ole Susanna.

The door opened just as Ethan was about to have an epic meltdown, and Annie walked in carrying a casserole dish and a pitcher of tea.

"Susanna, hun, I made you some tater tot casserole and sweet tea. I heard you gave K.C. quite the scare."

Just Annie saying K. C's name made the vein on the right side of Ethan's head bulge so far out I thought it was going to burst. Annie never even acknowledged Ethan but, like a mamma bear, her instincts were that I wanted him gone.

"Susanna do not forget that it's Monday. I let you lay around all day to feel better, but now it's time to get up and come clean my house. I have my Monday night book club in an hour so the sooner the better, hun. If you aren't down in ten minutes, expect one mad landlord to be back up here." And just like that Annie was gone.

Ethan was raging mad. He knew he'd just been beaten by a woman wearing overalls and I was not going back with him. His hardened eyes looked at me as he left, and he said, "I already told you this once you will not survive without me, Susanna. We both know it. Good Luck."

I fought back tears and stood face to face with him. I did not back down. He left, knowing he'd lost.

I looked back at the table with the food and felt genuinely taken care of. Annie was kind-hearted as much as she put up a front. I went downstairs to where she was working in her yard.

"Annie, I just want to say thanks."

She interrupted me, "No need. We have a business deal. You don't have to clean today. It's already too late. Go back up and eat your supper."

Overwhelmed by the events of the last few days, tears filled my eyes. Without a thought I hugged Annie. She stiffened like a board but allowed me to hold on a little longer than she seemed comfortable with.

"Go on now. Go eat, and I will see you in the morning."

~

I headed off to the shop early. Ian and Kat's wedding was the Saturday. I decided I wasn't going to worry about pleasing the mayor and her expectations but that I was going to make everything perfect for Ian and Kat. Every little detail was going to have my absolute attention.

I was writing down all the supplies I would need, when a man walked in. His demeanor was awkward. He had a beard and glasses that kept falling down his nose. He looked around as if someone were watching him, and I got a nervous feeling in my stomach just by his presence.

"Good morning. Can I help you with something?"

"I would like to send one, single red rose to someone."

"Ok, I can do that. Who am I delivering this to?"

"Deliver to Sara at the city hall. I want the card to read 'Wink, wink.'"

I looked up at the awkward man and tried to hide my nervousness. I did not know what Richard Gram looked like, but from the sound of his voice on the phone, he was not what I had imagined.

"Ok, Mr....?

"I am paying with cash. How much?" he said in the same paranoid way he was looking around.

He paid then left, and I wondered if Sara's secret wasn't a secret. Was that man her husband? Could that have been Richard Gram?

On my way to deliver the bud vase, I saw K.C. heading into the café. He looked at me and waved. I was hoping he would ask me to breakfast, but ever since he'd thought he did me in with his handsome looks and heavenly smile he had not acted the same way.

I walked into the city hall, and there was Sara. She looked up, surprised to see me.

"Hi, Susanna. You have a delivery for someone?"

"It's for you, Sara. I will put it right here on the counter." I wanted to leave before the mayor saw me.

"Sara?" I heard her. "Sara, please tell Ms. Hightower to come to my office. I need to speak with her."

Sara looked up at me as she read the card then looked at the single red rose. It was not the grand gesture of the dozen red roses sent before, and she seemed confused.

She asked, "Who sent this?"

"I…I don't know. I am not…. I am just the messenger."

The blood from Sara's face was leaving, and she stammered, "Is this a joke? Susanna, are you being cruel? You have no idea what you do not know."

"Sara, I have no idea what you are talking about."

Sara was glaring at me when the mayor, aggravated with my not being in her office, yelled, "SARA!" Sara didn't even acknowledge her and just continued to look for answers in my face.

"I'm just the messenger," I again said and headed to the mayor's office.

"Ms. Hightower, how are you feeling? Ian told me you had an episode."

"Yes ma'am, I had a severe migraine. I am better now."

"Well good, because this week will be a big week and I need all hands-on deck. Are you prepared for Saturday?"

"Yes. I will start working Friday so that all the blooms are fresh for Saturday afternoon."

"Oh, Susanna, I hope you aren't cutting it too close with that timeline. Everything needs to be done by 10:00 A.M. so family portraits can begin at 11:00 A.M. The ceremony will start precisely at 1:00 P.M. sharp. And do not forget the photographer will be there by 8:00 A.M. to start documenting the day. Please wear something that coordinates with the color scheme. We don't want to look back at the photos and all we see is the florist sticking out. That would be an awful waste of money spent on the photographer.

"I have the final table schematics ready for you so you know exactly where each arrangement is to be placed, which bridesmaids receive which bouquet, and which ones the mothers will be carrying.

"SARA!" she yelled. "Print out another copy of the finalized wedding plan." After Sara didn't answer, she screamed again. "I swear that girl was taken by aliens this weekend, and all they left me was her body. I do not need this scatter-brained nincompoop this week."

Sara didn't answer a second time, causing the mayor to leave her office. She slammed the door behind her, and I could hear her screeching at Sara. She came back with a stack of papers and handed them to me.

"Here. This is written in such detail that a monkey could put this wedding together."

I laughed to myself and wanted to say, "I see one already did."

It was as if the mayor could read my mind because she squinted her baby blue eyes as if to say, "Shut it, flower lady, and get busy." I took that as my cue to leave.

"Good day, Mayor Gram. I will see you Saturday."

~

I got back to the shop ready to start wedding preparations while checking my messages, I had a call from the local funeral home. They had a funeral coming in, and the family wanted to speak with me about doing the casket and family arrangements.

I got a lump in my throat because when the thought of opening a flower shop entered my mind, the only thoughts I had were of making flowers that people sent when they were madly in love. I thought about seeing the look on someone's face when they received "Congratulations on your baby" flowers. I did not think through people sending flowers when people died.

l reluctantly called back the funeral home and agreed to meet later on with the family.

The family arrived in the shop shortly after lunch. A grief-stricken husband who looked like his whole world just ended walked into my old building, and it was as if the walls knew something I didn't, a chill shivering once again down my spine.

"Susanna? I am Judge Greg Dillon, county judge here in Cartman. My wife Felicia passed away suddenly last night, and I need to order—" He uncontrollably started crying as his daughters held him and told him it was going to be okay.

I had never witnessed family love like this, and I felt awkward. I didn't know what to say, and I sure as hell didn't know how to help make this better. There sat at my table all together a man, his daughters and his sister who was obviously the back bone right now. Yet the tension between them could be felt along with the love. I was not sure what emotion was stronger, grief or animosity.

"My brother is clearly not in a state of mind to be ordering flowers, Susanna. Do you have any suggestions?" *Run, run away and never look back. Get on a plane and run straight back to Ethan and be the quitter you are. Life is*

easier that way.

"I…well, it is very endearing to see a man so much in love. So how about red roses? Beautiful, perfect red roses to say, 'I will love you forever.'"

"Well, that sounds extravagant and expensive," the woman replied.

"My sister does not share the same love I have for my wife. Roses sound perfect."

"Greg, the charade of being a perfect couple can end now. Now you have a chance at a new life. Felicia is not— was not—ever worthy of your love."

Was this argument really happening? This poor lady was not even cold, and her sister in law was condemning her forever.

"Roses please, Susanna. And please spare no cost," replied Judge Dillon. "The service will be tomorrow night, so if you can have those delivered to the funeral home by lunch tomorrow, I would be so appreciative."

As the judge and his daughters, along with his cold-hearted sister, walked out, K.C. walked in.

"Good to see you, Judge," said K.C. in a friendly voice.

"Hi K.C., how are you? I wish we could stay and catch up but, I am not sure if you heard, Felicia passed away last night, and I have to finish up." The judge, once again unable to control his emotions, broke down. With an emptiness, he hugged K.C. and said, "Please tell your family. I am not sure your sister even knows yet."

K.C. stood there, caught off guard, and for the first time he appeared to not have his thoughts in order.

"Hi K.C. Can I help you with something today?" He just stared blankly at me.

"Well, I came in to order some flowers but I just…the judge? His wife? I mean, I just saw Felicia at my sister's…at the mayor's birthday dinner the other night. The pain Greg is going to feel just makes me want to runaway"

"Were your families close, I mean I guess when you belong to such prominent people in the community your families have to be close?"

K.C. did not answer he was lost and seemed truly heart broken by the passing of Judge Dillon's wife.

"Yes? Our families were very close.

"Susanna do you want…do you want to go fishing with me, I mean I came in here needing flowers but I just…I need to get away and clear my head, so would you like to go with me…fishing?"

Fishing? I thought to myself.

"Sure?" I replied, questioning both his proposal and my answer.

~

I had no idea how to fish, but there I sat on the banks of the pond—or as they were referred to in Cartman, Texas, "the banks of the tank." I wasn't about to take my eyes off of the little red and white ball bobbin' there in the water, but what the hell was I watching for?

K.C. was a natural fisherman, the way he effortlessly cast his line and smoothly reeled in the fish. It was the same way he reeled people in...effortlessly, gently. Reeling me in just like a fish, I was hooked.

The afternoon sun was reflecting off the water, my skin was soaking in the heat of the Texas day, and the smell of a nearby peach tree filled the air. This was the life I imagined when I left New York. This was the man I had been dreaming about since I was a girl.

I felt like a girl when I was with him, like a silly little girl, and I wanted to feel like a woman. I wanted to be his woman. I wanted to be in his arms, but I wanted to run away at the same time. My life was not meant to be here. Here was too perfect. The life I escaped from was full of imperfections. That was where I belonged. For the first time, I desperately wanted to return to the dark shadows of Ethan.

"Susanna! Your bobber! You have a fish!"

"Holy hell, I have a fish! Now what?"

"REEL, SUSANNA! REEL!" Suddenly K.C. was behind me, helping me. I felt his body up against mine, and I was lost in his arms.

I dropped the rod and turned around, and for the first time we were face to face. His scent was too much for me to run from anymore.

He looked down at me, and I was not certain if it was a look of yearning or a look of distain.

"Susanna, I can't." My heart stopped beating for a moment. "I am not who you think I am. I gave my heart away a long time ago, and the woman I gave it to left me and took it with her. I only exist as a shell of a man."

"K.C., I didn't mean to make you uncomfortable. It's been an emotional day. I am sorry. I shouldn't have…" As I held my tears back, uncontrollable laughter started. "I guess I lost the fish. Suppose I owe you dinner now."

K.C. laughed in return, but the moment—my idiotic moment of daydreaming about a cowboy making love to me on the banks of a pond on a hot Texas day like in some damn country song—was too much to handle. He laughed and politely suggested we pack up and head back into town. The sun was setting, and my dreams of a perfect life were getting as dark as the night sky without the stars to wish upon.

We drove back in silence. I was dreading driving into the driveway and the awkward second of saying goodbye, when the headlights shone on my tiny apartment over the garage.

"Susanna," he said in an apologetic way, "I don't think you fully understand. It's truly not you. When I am with you, my heart…my heart starts to flutter and my body starts to ache, and I just…I just want to take you in my arms and never let go. But I made a promise, and I fucking keep my promises. But your smile makes me want to break every damn promise I ever made."

"Susanna, I can't love you, but I can't not love you." Before I knew what was happening, I could taste his lips and feel his chest, his heart beating against mine. And for the first time in my entire life I felt as if I did not want to run.

~

I woke up the next morning praying that the night before was not a dream. I checked my phone, but there were no messages. My heart sunk.

I can't love you, but I can't not love you. I kept replaying those words repeatedly in my head. What did he mean by that? Was K.C. married? He said he made a promise. He sent flowers to a special lady who had his heart. He said he gave his heart away and never got it back.

I had never in my life been so confused, and mad, but I was not sure who I was mad at. Myself, for falling for a smooth-talking, cheating cowboy? K.C., for playing with my emotions? Or the woman who had his heart and didn't seem to care that she had broken it into a million tiny pieces?

I did not have time for my own love story. I needed to make a beautiful arrangement of roses for a man who'd just lost his wife, and I had to deliver it to the funeral home before lunch. Then I had to start Ian and Kat's wedding arrangements. My heart ached for the judge who was about to say goodbye to the love of his life as another couple was about to begin their life together. I was angry—angry that life played such awful tricks on the heart.

That morning I made sure each rose was perfect in shape and color and smell, and I delicately arranged each one to cascade together in perfect harmony as if they were but one single rose, confessing its undying love.

I was nervous walking into the funeral home and a bit scared as the old Victorian style funeral home wall seemed to know more than the walls of shop and the walls here didn't dance to their own song but instead wept endlessly. As I approached the room where Felicia was, I heard the sobs of a woman. There was the mayor, leaning over the body of Felicia Dillon, holding onto her. I had never seen a dead body, and I sure as hell had never seen someone holding a dead body up out of a casket.

I was frozen when a frail lady beside me said, "They were 'special' friends."

Just then K.C. came from the other side of the room and grabbed the mayor. I heard him tell her that it was time to let go now and that the family was on their way.

As they turned to leave, we all three made eye contact. K.C. looked away as fast as he could. The mayor, however, looked right through me. Her eyes were lifeless, and I am muttered, "I'm sorry."

She stepped back, regaining her senses. Suddenly, she was aware that I knew her secret.

I knew her secret, her scandalous secretary's secret, her cheating husband's secret. I never knew the small-town florist would know all the dirty little secrets of the town.

And the thought of having to keep them started to make me feel like I did the day the weed killer tried to kill me.

~

K.C. met me at the door of my shop, and before I could tell him to leave and that I wanted nothing to do with him or his family or this messed up town, he grabbed me by the waist and into his arms, and again I melted. Nothing else mattered.

"Susanna, things here in Cartman aren't as you might have thought. This town is full of skeletons in closets, and most of them belong to my family."

No shit, I thought to myself.

"Will you go somewhere with me?" he asks. I really wanted to book a flight back to New York, but my attraction to K.C. gave way to all my good senses.

"K.C., I don't know. I can't even begin to process what I just saw at the funeral home, and I just…I don't know. Where do you want to go?"

"I need to take you somewhere. Please just come with me, Susanna. I know what you saw doesn't make sense, and I know I have you wanting to go back to New York. But before you leave me, please, I beg you come with me."

I did not have the power to leave K.C. Not at that moment and probably not ever.

We drove outside of town and, as we approached a gated entrance, K.C. turned pale.

"Susanna, please do not judge me."

We pulled into the most beautiful land I had ever seen. Trees larger and grander than any building in New York. And as we made our way up a hill, the statues and monuments that surrounded us were comforting and peaceful.

Suddenly, I was very aware of where we were.

We stopped, and I cautiously got out of the truck and followed K.C to a headstone.

"Lydia Rose Gram ~ Beloved Wife"

I began to cry uncontrollably as I looked up at K.C. How could he ever love me? A weed, literally amongst a Rose.

"Susanna, Rose was the first girl I ever kissed. We were in seventh grade at the homecoming dance, and she laughed so hard she snorted. I gave her my heart that night and we were inseparable until…" He choked back tears and proceeded to tell me a love story that movies are made of.

"Rose was out running one morning when a car swerved off the road and hit her. She was killed on impact, and they never caught the suspect. I was supposed to be with her that morning, but I was working in Austin at the time. Rose begged me to come home because she missed me, but I was a different person back then and my priorities were so jacked up. I made a promise to never put anything before her ever again. Until you, Susanna. As I try to focus on taking deeps breaths, so my knees don't buckle, K.C. continues to talk and my body won't stop shaking.

"The moment I saw you my whole world was turned upside down. I hated myself for having these feelings, but I meant it when I said you brought beauty to this town. I really meant you brought beauty again to my life."

He pulled me in and wiped my tears.

"Please take me home, K.C. I am not beautiful. I do not bring beauty to the town, and I sure as hell can't bring it to your life. I am weed, K.C. That's all I am. Sometimes weeds have blossoms but, underneath, they are still just a weed that needs to be gone for the roses to bloom. Please take me home."

~

That night I cried until I couldn't cry anymore. What was I doing in this town? I didn't belong here. I was not sure where I belonged.

The buzz from my phone startled me as I was pondering my next move. It was Ethan. Somehow, he always knew that when I needed him the least was when he could affect me the most.

"What do you want, Ethan? It's late and I am in no mood."

"Well, it's good to hear your voice too, Susanna."

"Seriously, Ethan, what?"

"Susanna, I miss you. I miss your face, your laugh, the way you hold me tight at night when the world around me is crumbling. You are my safe haven, and I have been a bully to you. I will give you the world if you come back to me. I promise, I am done with all the stupid kid shit. I want to be your man. I want to be your cowboy."

DO.NOT. FALL. FOR. THIS. SUSANNA. Why now? Why is he saying all the right things now? His instinct for my weakness was definitely his superpower.

"Ethan, I have waited so long for you to say these words, but that's all they are…words. A man, a real man— a cowboy—he is a man of few words and massive action. A boy uses words to get what he wants, and that's all you are, Ethan. A boy."

He laughed his cocky laugh. "Susanna, this is your last chance with me. I will let you come back to me or I will prove to you what this 'boy' is capable of. Don't come back and you will regret it."

"Is that a threat, Ethan?"

"Oh Susanna, no sweetheart, that is a promise."

I hung up the phone, scared once again. Ethan's temper was nothing to be messed with when his narcissism was out of control. I had just called him a boy, and to Ethan, being called a boy was justification for whatever retaliation he had in mind.

A knock on the door about made me jump out of my skin, and I was surprised to see Annie.

"Hey hun, I noticed your light on and, well, I talked to K.C. earlier. I just…well, I just wanted to check on you and talk with ya a bit, if that's ok. I brought cake. You put on some coffee and we are going to get some things worked out. Annie moves about the loft busy plating the cake and I wondered in that moment if this was what it was like to have a real mom, one who bakes cakes for you when you are sad. I bet Annie was a good mom because she is a good friend.

"Susanna, you need to understand K.C. has been through so much over the past few years, from the death of our mother to the death of his wife." OUR MOTHER???? Did Annie just say our mother? Annie and K.C and the mayor are siblings. Just when I thought life was more complicated than I could ever imagine I find out my friend, my soul mate and my enemy all come from the same blood and blood is always thicker than water.

"When you passed out in front of him it scared him to the core, so much so that he said any woman whom he loved was cursed and he would not curse you with his love. My brother is the most wonderful man there is besides my daddy. Daddy and K.C. are angels here on Earth and, sadly, their goodness has caused a lot of grief in their lives.

"Daddy was the mayor; did you know that? Before Gina, Daddy was the mayor of Cartman. The town adored Daddy. K.C was set to follow in his footsteps and was working in Austin as an intern for a law firm specializing in land and water rights. K.C. and Daddy were going to save

the farmers and protect their rights from big government

corruption.

"Rose begged K.C. to take some time off and come

home. She was ready to start a family. K.C. was in love

with Rose but his devotion to Daddy and their quest for real

change outweighed that love. He blames himself for Rose's

death. You know they never caught who did it, who ran her

over? I have my theories though."

Annie, in the dim light of my apartment lamp, was

visibly shaking. She seemed to be nervous about

something, or maybe gaining up enough courage to say

what she wanted to say next

"Susanna, there is nothing more valuable here than

land and water. People for years have fought, sacrificed,

and died to protect both. The Cartman family has owned

most of the land here for generations, and there are people

working day and night to take it out from under us. K.C. vowed to protect it, but when Rose was killed," she immediately corrected herself, "when Rose died, he vowed to never put anything or anyone in front of her. And then you came.

"K.C. needs you, Susanna. This town needs you. Whatever your heart feels tonight, it's okay, but I beg you as your friend to please stay in Cartman."

What did she mean this town needed me? Annie herself didn't want me here, and now, suddenly, the town needed me? And Rose wasn't just killed, but murdered?"

"Susanna, I know I overwhelmed you, hell I overwhelmed myself just now thinking about everything that has happened to my family to my brother and sister ...to me. I'm sorry. I hope you...well, enjoy the rest of the cake. I have to go finish some paper work."

I was hoping I was in the middle of some weird, late-night, snack-induced dream, but when my phone rang and it was K.C., I knew the only dream I was in was the dream of a perfect life with him.

"Hi," he said, and I could hear his voice crack on the other end. "I wanted to call and check on you. I was afraid you might get a migraine after all I told you today. I needed to hear your voice and know you are alright."

"Hey, K.C. I am fine. Thanks for calling. I am not going to lie; my head is spinning. Annie just left and we had a long talk. I don't understand everything that has gone on or is going on with you and your family, and I'm not sure I want to. All I know is I feel safe around you. We all have pasts, we all have secrets that we try and overcome, and sometimes we do a really good job at pretending to be okay with who we are.

"I was okay pretending to be a small-town florist, pretending to live in this perfect little town, pretending to be in love with a man who gave his heart to someone else, but all of that changed today because my love for you is real and I can't pretend anymore here. So, I either I have to leave and find a new place to be a new person or stay and show the real me. The thought of you seeing who I really am, though, scares the shit out of me. I am afraid after you see the real me that I will no longer feel safe around you."

"Susanna, you can be brave and afraid at the same time. Trust me, I have been doing it my whole life. Can I come over?"

Brave and afraid at the same time, I thought… "Yes!"

That night I let my superficial guard down for the first time ever. To be brave and afraid at the same time is how I'd lived my life. Brave enough to leave a man who destroyed me bit by bit, but afraid enough of what would happen after I left that I considered too many times going back. Brave enough to leave my family and the only way of life I had ever known, but too afraid to do it on my own. I was brave enough to show K.C. who and what I was, and afraid he would leave the moment he found out.

He erased those fears with a simple kiss on the forehead. Not the passionate kiss of lovers, but the empathetic kiss of one soul connected to another. A kiss that reminded me I was worthy of affection and love. A kiss of safety. It was brave and afraid at the same time. It was the kiss that made me want to stay and face tomorrow with K.C., whatever that may bring.

~

I woke up with a hangover. The kind you get from crying and thinking and talking. It was Friday, the day before Ian and Katherine's wedding, and I had so much to do. But all I could think about was how drastically my life had changed in twenty-four hours.

I met K.C. at the café for breakfast. The smile on his face was refreshing, and I couldn't help but smile from the inside. Nothing and no one were going to ruin my day.

Then I looked up and in walked Mayor Gram.

"Susanna, hope you are fueling up to get all your work done. I can only imagine what a busy little bee like you has to do today besides spending the morning with the local feed store owner." She glances at K.C. "Brother, good to see you this morning." Her voice toward K.C. was just as condescending as it was to me and everyone else around her.

My disdain for the mayor was growing immensely. She looked at the people of her town like they were trash carried in the wind from the dump. Why would anyone elect her to represent them? I could see her marble mansion, City Hall, out the window of my historic building, and I couldn't help but wonder how a town so small and so old could ever afford the cost to build such a prestigious building. Something did not make sense; it just did not add up.

I would have loved to uncover some scandalous ties to the mayor— a wealthy businessman who funded the building under the table as the mayor padded her silk-lined pockets. Oh, a girl could dream of taking someone as slithery as the mayor down. But the fact of the matter was I was merely a florist. The only florist in a one horse, one light, one-sided town. If there was a scandal, it would come out eventually, and when it did, I wanted to be the first one to visit the witch in prison and see her trade in her expensive couture clothing for an orange jumpsuit.

I looked up at Mayor Gram and remembered how just a few short hours ago she'd been draped over the dead body of Felica Dillon, the county judge's wife, unconsolably sobbing at the loss of her special friend. And now it was as if it never happened. She was impeccably put together and did not appear to have shed a tear. I was almost envious of her lack of empathy and her cold heart.

"Mayor Gram, I am indeed fueling up. No need to worry yourself, Ian and Katherine's wedding"—I made sure to emphasize whose wedding it was— "will be as perfect as they are together."

She smirked and replied, "Oh, Susanna dear, perfection is unreal, shallow even, and oftentimes fatally uninteresting. Well, I must go. I just came in to tell my brother not to forget about family portraits in the morning."

And just like that she sucker punched me in the gut again and was out of reach before I had my wits back. I looked at K.C, waiting to be acknowledged for the abuse I had received, but all I got in return was a pity laugh and a shake of the head.

"Susanna, one word of advice: My sister always gets the last word. We both have law degrees and we've both won numerous debate awards, but she has one more than I do and it's the one from when we debated each other. She wins at all cost. My sister always has the last word. It's her gift."

I couldn't believe it. Was he taking up for her? Her gift was the gift of being a cold-hearted bitch?

I didn't have time to analyze the messed-up family bond between K.C. and his sister. I had a wedding to prepare for and it was going to be anything but fatally uninteresting.

I checked my messages as I always did, first thing, and the only message I had was from Richard Gram. *Not today, Richard. Please not today*, I cried.

"Yes, I need a dozen roses sent to Sara at city hall. Just sign the card "Wink wink" and charge the card you have on file. Also, send one long-stem, yellow rose to Mayor Gram. Sign the card 'To my yellow rose of Texas. Love, Richard.'"

I couldn't believe it. There I was preparing for Ian and Katherine's wedding. I sat looking at all the beautiful blooms surrounding me, the purple anemone capturing my attention and I recalled a story I read when searching for all the flowers and their origins. Greek mythology tells the famous love story of Aphrodite and Adonis. According to the myth, Aphrodite's ex-lover, Ares, grew jealous of her affair with Adonis and disguised himself as a boar and attacked Adonis, killing him. Legend has it that Aphrodite hurried to Adonis, but his soul had already left him. In despair, she sprinkled nectar on his wounds, and as she carried her lover's body out of the woods, crimson anemones sprung up where each drop of blood fell onto the ground.

The sight of this flower in all its beauty, without any scent of its own, gave me an unsettling feeling as if it were a warning sign. All love triangles end with someone's nectar and blood falling to the earth, and I was in the middle of a love triangle that wasn't even my own.

~

I delivered the flowers to city hall. There was Sara, as meek and mild as ever, sitting at the front desk.

"Hi, Susanna. How are you today?" she squealed.

I wanted to walk past her and take all the flowers to the mayor. I wanted her to be crushed at the thought that they were not for her. I wanted her feelings to be hurt the same way mine were hurt when I found out K.C. had given his heart away to someone else. Why did I hate her so much for betraying the mayor? Especially since it appears the mayor was having an affair of her own. I loathed

Regina Gram, but somewhere deep down I felt this odd, protective connection to her.

I confused her momentarily by asking for the mayor before handing her the flowers. It was worth it to see the blood drain from her face before telling her the dozen red roses signed by "wink wink" himself were hers. *For crying out loud, come up with something less adulterous than "wink wink."*

"The mayor is out right now," Sara said as she gazed like a school girl at her flowers.

"This delivery is for her. Can I leave it on her desk?"

"Yea sure. Go on back." She said as she stared at the yellow rose and looked back with less enthusiasm at her own flowers.

I walked into the mayor's office. It was a disheveled mess like I had not seen. It looked as if it had been ransacked. I looked for an empty spot on her desk, and that's when I accidently spilled one of the five coffee cups sitting around.

Son of bitch! I was frantically trying to dry off the papers when one of the documents grabbed my attention. It was a contract to purchase 2,100 acres on 989 Cartman Drive, to be sold to Greg Dillon.

The mayor was selling Cartman property to the judge. I did not know why but that did not seem right. Maybe it was the conversation I had with Annie the night before still in my head—how the Cartman's owned the majority of the property and how much K.C. loves the land—but I had an ache in my gut that told me K.C. was about to be blindsided by something.

I left the papers how they were, left the rose on top of them, and hurried out of the office. My heart was racing. I needed to get to K.C. as soon as possible.

I was heading down the sidewalk when I heard my name.

"Hey hey, Susy Q. Where ya headed? I was just coming in to talk to you." It was Kat, as bouncy as ever, drinking her green smoothie.

"Hey Kat. I was just headed to the feed store, but it can wait for the bride-to-be."

We walked into the shop and Katherine's demeanor immediately changed.

"Susanna," she said sternly. She had never said my name, and I was frightened to hear what she was about to say. "Susanna, do you know?"

"Do I know what?"

"Why I was going to leave Ian. You know the day you saw me and Regina leaving the bank? It's because she paid me fifty thousand dollars to leave Ian, to leave and never come back. She said their family legacy did not have room for trash like me and my family and that Ian deserved

someone who knew what being affluent meant. I took it. I

took the money and was going to leave because I believed

her.

"Susanna, I am pregnant. I don't know that I want

to raise a child who has Regina Gram as their grandmother.

Money isn't everything, but for a girl like me fifty thousand

is like winning the lottery. I could raise a child on that, and

Ian could find a girl not so rough around the edges to make

a life with."

Was this seriously happening? I thought the biggest

scandal of a small town would be who spray painted *I wuz*

here on the water tower. How in the hell did I find myself

in the middle of so much scandal? Judith Markley warned

me that the walls of this old building would not be the only

secret keepers of the town.

"Katherine. Do not let Regina Gram and her family 'legacy' take away the chance for you and Ian to make your own family legacy. A last name is just that, a last name. It doesn't make you who you are. It's not your legacy. The things you value and hold true to in this life, that's your legacy. A last name can be changed as easily as it was given.

"Your baby, though, he or she deserves the love only Ian can give them, and you deserve the love he has for you. Most importantly, he deserves to be loved by a woman who knows what the definition of family is. Do not let Regina Gram have the last word. When you say 'I do' tomorrow, she will no longer have a say.

"I recently received some of the best advice I have ever been given. You can be brave and afraid at the same time. So tomorrow, if you become afraid, you look for me. I will be your brave face overshadowing the fear of Regina

Gram. Together, Katherine, you and I will make sure Mayor Gram doesn't have the last word."

We hugged as genuine friends, and as Katherine walked out the door, I couldn't help but wonder when I got to the wedding venue tomorrow if Regina Gram would indeed still have the last word.

~

The morning of the wedding finally arrived, and I had never been more nervous in my whole life. But I felt prepared for anything the day was going to throw at me, and I headed to the cemetery to deliver Judith Markley's "state champion forever" arrangement to her husband. The sun was shining, the birds were singing, and it was going to be a wonderful day.

I found Mr. Markley's grave, and there, three rows over, was Lydia Rose Gram. I walked over to her, sat down, and left the arrangement K.C. had asked me to deliver—a beautiful arrangement without roses for someone special who had his heart. The card read, "To my dearest Lydia Rose, the flowers here on Earth are nothing compared to the Roses in Heaven. You will forever hold a piece of my heart, but it is time my heart to be at peace. XO, K.C."

As I sat the arrangement down, I felt guilty, like I was inflicting pain on a woman I'd never met. I wondered how Sara could look Mayor Gram in the eyes every day and not feel heartache over the pain she could cause her. I began to cry. All I could do was talk to the sky and tell Lydia I was sorry.

Driving back to town, I focused on all the details of the day. I stopped at the shop to load up all the arrangements, and there waiting at my door was Ethan. I was tempted to drive off, but I had to be brave and face him. I read somewhere that when face to face with a grizzly bear, you must make yourself as large as possible and stand your ground if you want any chance of survival, and that is what I intended to do…be so big that he would give up and leave me alone.

Shoulders back, chest out, I confidently confronted him at the door.

"Ethan, I do not have the time or the energy for anything you have to offer me. This town is small, but the café up the street has decent food and coffee. Other than that, I suggest you go back home."

As I was turning the key in the door of the old building, the familiar chill of the haunted walls sent a shiver up my spine. Just as I entered the doorway, Ethan grabbed my upper arm and pulled me into him. I tried to pull away, but he pulled me closer, his face so close to mine I could almost feel his kiss. He stared into my eyes and, normally, I look away like a punished child, but I stood my ground and stared back. After what seemed like an eternity, he pushed me away and walked out. He never said a word; he didn't have to. The coldness in his eyes said it all.

I felt the tears of fear coming up from my toes, Ethan wanted to hurt me…. He could have hurt me…. I was still not certain that he wouldn't.

~

Still shaken from the incident with Ethan I managed to have everything prepared for the wedding when I heard "These flowers and arrangements are kind of fatally uninteresting, don't you think?"

I quickly turned to see K.C. and my breath left my body. He had on a crisp white shirt, unbuttoned at the collar, black slacks, and his cowboy hat. I had only ever seen cowboys in old Western movies, and I never understood the appeal. They were usually dirty, playing poker, and drinking whiskey. I was not sure if it was hat or the smile that caused every inch of my skin to become electrified, but whatever it was, that man had me and there was no turning away from it.

"Susanna, everything is absolutely beautiful but truly fails in comparison to the florist who made it all possible."

"K.C. Cartman you are one smooth talker and you might just end up having to dance with the hired help before the night is over.

In his snarky but charming way he replied, "Pending permission granted by the mayor also my name is Kole Cartman, K.C for short."

"Oh, I beg of your forgiveness, I should know better than to not know the name of the mayor's brother." I rolled my eyes and laughed.

Just then, as if on cue, I heard her familiar, condescending voice. When I looked up, I couldn't believe my eyes.

There in the August summer sun of Texas stood the mayor in a layered, black lace dress that looked as if she had just stepped off a stagecoach from one of those Western movies—black bonnet with a black veil and, yes, a black parasail. She had the audacity to tell me to wear something nice so that I didn't ruin the pictures but thought this was perfectly acceptable. I didn't know whether to laugh out loud or run and tell Katherine to get out while she still could, that no one in their right mind should willingly be a part of this kind of drama.

While barking orders at the wait staff, clearly not concerned with what people would say of her attire, she turned, and the ice-cold chill of her blue eyes landed on me.

"Susanna, do you have everyone's bouquets ready? It is time for family portraits.

"I do. I have them at the front, under the arch way. Everything has a label so there should not be any confusion. I tried to make it so easy a monkey could do it."

I waited for her punch my throat with her comeback, but as I braced myself for a knockout, I was stunned by what I heard in return…silence. Nothing. Had I just gotten in the last word? Did someone finally beat Regina Gram? I was afraid to look at her, but I braved my fate and looked her in the eyes.

She just squinted in frustration and walked away. As K.C air high fived me and followed behind her, towards the family.

I began to laugh uncontrollably. I laughed so hard I snorted; I may have even danced a little jig.

Mid-celebration, I was startled by the shadow of a man. It was the man who came into my shop and ordered the single rose for Sara.

He watched me without any emotion and then said, "The mayor told me to tell the florist that a monkey must have taken the labels off the arrangements because they do not know who gets what."

I stared blankly at him, wondering if I was actually face to face with Richard Gram.

While trying, in my head, to figure out what was going on and who this man was, he smiled and said, "I am Brother Parks, Landon Parks, pastor at the 1st Baptist Church. But today I am the photographer. Don't worry, though, I won't shoot you—wink wink. Anyway, the mayor is requesting your service."

Did he just say, 'wink wink'? I felt as if I were running, but I looked down and my legs were not moving.

My heart was racing, and my mind was searching for answers to questions that I wasn't sure I'd even asked."

I quickly headed over to the mayor, only to find her in deep conversation with a man who I'd assumed was the infamous Richard Gram, but as he turned around, I recognized him. It was Judge Dillon.

I walked up to the two, and he politely said, "Good to see you again, Susanna. Felicia's flowers were the epitome of our love for one another and the most beautiful way I could have said goodbye.

"Regina"—he turned to the mayor— "we *will* continue this conversation," he said in an authoritative voice. The mayor seems to cower at his command.

"Susanna," she said as she reclaimed her wits, "the judge will be performing the ceremony today and was going over how I wanted things to proceed." It was if she were trying to justify her conversation with the judge to me. Clearly, by her demeanor, it was more than when he should announce them husband and wife.

"I am just here because the pastor—or the photographer—said that you didn't know which flowers yours were."

"What are you talking about?" she replied. "You told me you made it so that a monkey could figure it out and, well, Susanna, even Katherine figured it out. She handed out everyone's bouquets way before you came over to save the day. It's handled."

Thinking this day could not get any worse, I couldn't imagine why Brother Parks would tell me such a thing had it not come from the mayor herself. Then again, he had also joked that he wouldn't shoot me, and then with a smirk said, 'WINK WINK.' What the hell did that mean?

I did not have the mental capacity to process everything. I had to show up and pretend to be the biggest florist for the biggest wedding this town had ever seen, or I would be forced to pack up the life I thought I was creating here and move backward into a life I wanted to forget.

I looked at the time: thirty minutes left until the ceremony. The Texas heat was beating down like it had something to prove. It was so hot the icing was melting off of the cake, and the once crisp, white roses that adorned the backsides of the chairs were wilting and turning brown like the leaves in the fall. They looked how I felt. I'd started out confident and pure, but the heat, the dramatics, and the mayor had drained the water from me, wilted me, causing me to dry up and blow away in the hot, Texas wind. I did not think I could handle the rest of the day.

I was about to cry when K.C. walked up. Seeing his face was the water I needed to continue.

"Hey beautiful, you look like someone stole your thunder. Need me to go beat them up?" He grinned. I chuckled and rolled my eyes as he beat me to the punch. "Yes, I might even take a whack at my sister, if I have to."

"Oh, your sister is fine. I am not sure why she is hell-bent on being a bitch to me, but I have been treated worse by people far more powerful than her."

"Suse, my sister…she was not always like this. There is a lot about Gina that people don't know. She used to be full of life and love. Things just happened, and she had to become a woman in a man's world. You would have liked my sister ten years ago. Ya'll might have been friends."

Just as I was about to tell K.C. about the land contract I saw on the mayor's desk for the sale of Cartman property, Ian ran up, tears welling in his eyes.

"Uncle K.C, she's gone. Kat's gone! All that she left was a note saying she would love me always. Uncle Kole she is my everything. I don't want life without Katherine. I don't know what I did wrong. I just do not understand."

Ian's heartbreak was devasting, but what was worse was my needing to tell him why Katherine left.

"Ian…Ian I don't know how to say this, but I know why Katherine left."

I told him the whole story from the day of their birthdays, seeing them leave the bank, and about the money the mayor paid Katherine to leave.

Ian went from a heartbroken groom to a mad as hell man.

"Susanna, I truly appreciate you telling me everything, and I am sorry. You will more than likely suffer the repercussions for doing so after I confront my no-good, lying mother. I do hope you find a way to survive this, but Katherine isn't just my soulmate and best friend; she is my laughter, my tears, my heartache, and my happiness all in one. I will do whatever it takes to have her in my life."

Ian left to confront his mother, and K.C was there with him they looked like soldiers going to war, brothers in arms. I slowly began to take down the garlands of flowers and tiny white lights. *Wow! What a way to end what was to be such a celebratory day.*

I looked up to see Brother Parks taking pictures of everyone tearing down a wedding that was not going to happen. Why would he be documenting the moment in time Ian Gram would never want to remember?

"You know, today was supposed to celebrate the marriage vows taken by Ian and Katherine and honor the marriage of Mayor Gram and her faithfully loving husband, Richard, using their picture-perfect marriage as an example of what it takes to have a strong relationship." He said as he continued snapping pictures of guests leaving, the empty gift table, and caterers loading cases of champagne back into their delivery trucks. "Funny how the things we come to expect end up being very different from our expectations, great as they may have been." His voice was monotone, and his face was lifeless, but his words were full of emotion.

"I am not sure what you mean, but I do believe in love. I believe Ian and Katherine will have their love story; they just have to slay a few dragons first.

"HA! I do not believe in love stories, Mrs. Hightower. I believe our stories are what we make them, our choices. We choose who we love, how we love, and when we love. I do not believe we fall in love. People who fall are usually careless and not paying attention to their surroundings. I am not careless, and I pay very close attention, Mrs. Hightower, to every single detail." He snaps one last photo of me holding a handful red roses that moments before I had meticulously placed in vases, with the flash I was startled and dropped one single rose to the ground, and again I felt uncertain of what was to come.

When I looked up to tell him to stop taking photos, he was gone before the words could come off my tongue.

I could hear in the distance Ian lashing out at his mother. I packed up the last of my supplies, and as I closed the door to the car, Annie walked over.

"Oh, hey Annie. You look beautiful." She stood there in her baby blue skirt and blazer, her hair bigger than ever, and smelling like she'd just stepped out of a field of vanilla. I had grown to love Annie. She had become a friend, and I trusted her with my life.

"Hey, hun. Not the day we had thought it was going to be, huh?

"No ma'am, not at all. How are you?"

"Oh, you know me. I am an old pro at the dramatics of my sister and her family. How are you? Has she unleashed her wrath on you yet? K.C. told me you were the one to tell Ian about his mother's plans. He is still giving her a dose of her own medicine, but, hun, when she heals up, my sister will have you in her target. It's nothing actually personal toward you, but Regina has grown accustomed to winning at all costs. And you may have just cost her her only son."

"Annie, I need to tell you something else. I am not sure how to even…or if …I could be just…"

"Hun, the best way to tell someone something is just to start, without holding anything back."

I took a deep breath.

"Richard Gram has been sending Sara, Regina's secretary, roses and just signs the card 'wink wink' and told me not to say anything. The other day he sent Sara a dozen red roses—and you know when a man sends a woman a dozen red roses it is to symbolize his love for her—but he also sent Regina a long-stem, yellow rose and signed the card something about her being his yellow rose of Texas. Well, when I delivered them, she was out of her office. I went in and, like the clutz I am, spilled coffee on some papers, but not just any papers. Annie, it was a sales contract for Cartman property. I think Regina is selling ya'll's land."

Annie's face turned ghost white.

"Susanna, have you told K.C any of this?"

"No. Between the wedding and everything that we have been through, I just wanted to get through today. I just wanted to dance with a cowboy and be kissed under the Texas stars. I wanted the damn love story, Annie. Instead, I find myself in the middle of a mess that will only end badly for me."

"Susanna, you have to tell K.C. as soon as possible. Go back to your shop, unload your items, and come home as soon as possible. Our family could lose everything, and this town will suffer more than you know if this sale goes through. I will help K.C. get things finished here then we will meet you at the house. "Susanna, I am sorry."

I looked at her in confusion.

"I am sorry the ad for this town was misleading. Cartman, Texas is a far cry from the peaceful, easy-living town we say it is. I am sorry you came here."

~

When the Texas sun starts to set, it's not a long, slow sunset. It gives you only a few moments to bask in its glory before the night sky takes over and the shadows of the evening lurk.

I was unloading boxes when I saw Ethan across the street; rather, I could hear him humming.

"Oh, Susanna, oh don't you cry for me…" The sound was like a ghost whispering in my ear. It was haunting and cold, and I was frightened. My nerves were already shot, and I was jumpy as could be. I kept waiting to look up and see the mayor come flying in on her broom, wearing her death dress for the wedding day.

I tried to ignore Ethan and not give him the satisfaction of acknowledgement, but before I knew it the humming was louder. The ghost whispers were no longer whispers but Ethan's whiskey breath on the back of my neck.

"Where's your cowboy?" he asked. "I thought he would be here at your beck and call, helping 'the purdy lady' out," he said, slurring his words while trying his best to imitate a Texas drawl. "You know, Susanna, underneath that cowboy hat of his, he is no different from any other man. See, men don't get a new game; they only get a new audience. Whichever heart-crossed lover he had before you that fell for all the 'yes ma'ams' and 'how do ya do's is sitting somewhere alone, wondering what she did wrong, when the truth is, he just got bored and it was time to 'mosey' on."

Ethan was beyond drunk. I wanted to run but he was blocking the doorway. I wanted to scream but there was no one around to hear me.

"Ethan," I broke down and, through tears, I began to beg. "Ethan, please leave me alone. Go back to New York and let me be, please, please, please."

"Oh, Susanna, now don't you cry," he said as he laughed. "I am not going back without you. Baby…" His tone turned, and now he was the one begging. Through drunken tears, he begged and pleaded, "Susanna, I am nothing without you. I will quit drinking. I won't work so many hours. Whatever you want I will give it to you. You want to stay here and be farmers? I will buy us a house. I will buy the whole god-forsaken town for you. Please, just be mine. Be mine forever. Please."

As Ethan was begging on his knees, holding me by the waist like a small child clinging to its mother, the clank of the cowbell on the door startled us. It was K.C. and Annie.

K.C rushed over and threw Ethan off from me in one quick move. Before I knew what was happening, Ethan had swung at K.C.

"STOP!" I cry. "K.C., please stop! Leave him alone!"

K.C. had Ethan down on the ground, and punch for punch I could see Ethan slowly losing the light in his eyes.

I let out a final scream, "KOLE!"

~

I looked down at the sea of red on the floor, not sure if it was the rose petals falling from the heartbroken arrangements from the wedding. I realized it was blood… blood coming from my body.

I glanced over at Annie who looked like someone had just been shot.

I saw Ethan with no life in his eyes.

I fell into K. C's arms. I could feel his heart beating—or was it my heart beating? Perhaps it was both of ours, beating as one.

"Susanna be brave. Be brave, Susanna," he kept saying until I no longer heard him.

The familiar whisper from the haunted walls of my hundred-year-old building sent chills up my spine. All I could hear in the distance was someone singing, "Oh, Susanna, oh don't you mess with me" as they walked into the shadows of Cartman, Texas.

#

Made in the USA
San Bernardino, CA
10 December 2019